Something
Missing

DARLENE HALLIDAY

Something Missing
Darlene Halliday

Published by Cava Consulting
info@dealingwithdifficultpeople.info

National Library of Australia
Cataloguing-in-publication data:

ISBN 978-0-9923579-5-5

This is a book of fiction. All of the characters and events portrayed in this novel are either products of the author's imagination or are used fictitiously.

This book is dedicated to my children, because without them, this book would not have been written.

Something Missing

Chapter 1

Jenny Carponi braced herself for the collision she instinctively knew was coming. Even though it was January and the weather was -20 ° F Jenny felt perspiration gathering on her forehead and her hands even though she wore leather gloves. She was warmly dressed in black lined woollen pants, heavy thigh-length black leather jacket and white wool scarf. On her feet were leather boots that reached almost to her knees. To the right of her, in the passenger seat sat her grandmother, Jane Robertson who was warmly dressed in a full-length navy wool coat, lilac wool scarf and gloves. She also wore leather boots.

Jane had phoned Jenny that Friday morning and asked if she could take her up to the hospital, so they could spend the afternoon visiting Jenny's husband Russ who was a patient in the Winnipeg General Hospital. Russ had become ill the weekend before. When he visited his doctor on Wednesday he was immediately sent to the hospital and admitted suffering from a serious case of viral pneumonia. Russ had phoned Jenny that morning to say he could have visitors other than his wife.

After a pleasant hospital visit with Russ, Jenny and her grandmother drove to Jenny's home where she planned to cook and serve dinner before taking her grandmother home. Overnight, the city had been hit with a heavy snowfall and the snow removal crews had been hard pressed to clear the streets of the tons of snow that had fallen. Under that snow was pure ice, so driving was very dangerous. The side streets were full of snow, ruts and ice. Only the major streets had been cleared by the time Jenny and her grandmother left the hospital. Jenny was fully aware of how treacherous the roads were that day, so she drove very carefully even though she found it difficult to drive on such slippery surfaces. She began to wonder whether she should have come out with the roads in such terrible condition.

After she made a right turn off Portage Avenue (that had been completely cleared of snow) and had driven a short distance on the side road towards her home, Jenny braked and stopped her car. Both she and her grandmother leaned forward as they observed a car careening towards them at a high rate of speed.

'The stupid idiot!' yelled her grandmother, 'Why's he speeding with conditions like this?'

In summer there would have been room for three lanes of traffic – one being a parking lane – the other two for traffic. But because of the recent snowfall there was only one and a half lanes available for actual traffic. The parking lane was to Jenny's left and she noticed that a car half way down the block was passing the parked cars taking up most of the available traffic area. Even though Jenny had the right-of-way, she stopped her car leaving three full car lengths in front of the parked cars to allow the speeding car to pull into the parking lane that would allow her to proceed safely down the street.

The street was very icy and had big icy ruts on it, but this did not seem to worry the driver of the oncoming vehicle. Jenny could see that the driver was travelling far too quickly for the road conditions. His car was bouncing all over the road as he hit the ruts. Jenny and her grandmother sat in her motionless car as they waited for the other driver to move over in front of the parked vehicles. At the last minute, the driver braked as he attempted to move his car into the parking lane. As he did so his car spun sideways still travelling at a high rate of speed towards Jenny's car. Jenny knew the vehicle was going to hit her car broadside. As soon as she realised what was going to happen she yelled a warning to her grandmother 'Brace yourself – he's going to hit us.'

Both occupants had their lap belts tightened. There were no shoulder harnesses or air bags in those days, but the lap belts did keep passengers from being propelled through the windshield. Jenny closed her eyes and prepared for the crash. The other vehicle hit so hard that even though Jenny was prepared for the crash she was propelled forward with great force. There was an ear-splitting noise as the two massive metal objects collided and Jenny and Jane were pelted with shards of glass as the windshield shattered. Then suddenly there was absolute silence.

Jenny knew she must have been knocked unconscious for a few seconds because the first thing she noticed when she regained consciousness was that she was draped over the steering wheel facing the driver's door. Her face and ribs hurt terribly as did her right knee. She tried to open her eyes but could only open her left one. Her right eye was held shut by the pressure of her face against the steering wheel. As she looked down she could see blood dripping onto her left knee below.

'This is going to ruin my slacks,' she thought just before she chastised herself by thinking, 'What a stupid thing to worry about. I've obviously been injured—and it really hurts!'

When she peered upward she could see the dash of the car, but that was all. She attempted to sit up but found she couldn't do so. She seemed glued to the wheel and ached all over. Her effort to move made the world spin. She felt terribly dizzy and nauseous and hoped she wasn't going to be sick.

Suddenly it occurred to her that her grandmother was also in the car. Had she been injured as well? She didn't hear any movement from that side of her car. Because Jenny was facing the opposite way, she couldn't check her grandmother's condition. Fighting consciousness and trying to forget about her own injuries she focused her attention on how her grandmother might be after the accident. Her grandmother was in her early seventies and was a tough old lady, but she too could have been badly injured.

As Jenny lay helplessly draped over the steering wheel, she was just about to ask her grandmother how she was when she heard a lap belt retracting and a car door opening. Then she heard a young woman's voice asking if anyone was hurt.

'Please call an ambulance. My granddaughter has been badly hurt.' *s*he heard her grandmother say as she climbed out of the car. Jenny assumed that her grandmother was not seriously hurt. She saw her own door open and a young woman peered at Jenny in horror.

'I'm going to call an ambulance.' she said to Jane. 'You stay with her while I do so, but don't move her - think she's been seriously hurt.' The young woman turned around and Jenny's grandmother took her place. Then all Jenny felt was blackness closing in on her.

Chapter 2

When Jenny woke up she peered around the room and identified from her surroundings that she was in a hospital room. She was lying on her back and panicked when she realised she couldn't move her head. The reason became clear as she lifted her right hand and felt the cervical collar around her neck. As she investigated further she found that bandages covered most of her lower face. The nurse in the Intensive Care Unit (ICU) seeing her move quickly came over to her side. Jenny tried to speak but her mouth was so sore and swollen that all that came out of her mouth were garbled words.

The nurse realising that the facial bandages made it hard for Jenny to communicate, said, 'You're in the Misericordia Hospital. Don't try to talk. We've put stitches in your lips and some of your teeth are damaged. We've also put you in a cervical collar until we're able to do X-rays of your neck, jaw, ribs and spine. We're going to take you up to X-ray soon to see if there's any damage to your neck and back.'

Soon an orderly arrived and whisked her bed into X-ray. After having her X-rays, Jenny was returned to her curtained-off area in ICU. The nurse who had attended her earlier asked, 'Do you feel up to having some visitors?' In Jenny's confused state she assumed that it must be Russ waiting to visit her – then remembered that he was still a patient in another hospital. Then she wondered if it was her grandmother. She couldn't nod her head because of the collar so she gave a mumbled 'Yes.' Soon her worried parents, Martha and Ian Harper, entered the room.

'Don't try to talk, Jenny.' said her mother as she leaned across Jenny's bed to give her a light peck on her forehead. Then she added, 'The nurse has told us that you have stitches in your lips, so they don't want you to talk. I know you're worried about your grandmother, but she's fine. She had a few stitches and the police drove her home. We'll keep an eye on her to make sure she's all right.' said Martha as she gave her daughter another light kiss on the forehead. 'We'll try asking you questions that you can answer with a 'yes' or a 'no.' One blink for 'yes', two for 'no.' Okay?'

Jenny blinked once, and they communicated as much as possible using that method.

'The police said that the other driver was speeding and hit you broadside. Is that correct?' asked her mother.

Jenny blinked once for 'yes.'

Was your car moving when you were hit?' Ian asked. Jenny blinked twice for 'no.'

'You were just coming home from seeing Russ at the hospital?' Martha queried.

Jenny blinked once for 'yes.'

'You're going to have two beautiful shiners.' said her father as he examined the bruising and discolouration on the top of her face, the part that wasn't covered with bandages.

'Later, we'll take your key and get some toiletries, a housecoat, socks and slippers for you. And we'll let Russ know that you're here.' Ian added.

Her parents turned as a doctor entered the room carrying several X-rays. 'Hello Jenny. I'm Dr. Warren. I'm the orthopaedic specialist on duty today. We've examined your X-rays and are concerned by the swelling in your spinal column, both in the neck area and between the fourth and fifth vertebrae in the lumbar region of your lower back. You'll have to wear the cervical collar until the neck swelling goes down.' he stated. He checked to see that Jenny was absorbing what he was saying, and then continued, 'I'm sure it hurts when you breathe. Two of your ribs were broken, so I'll tape them up soon. You were lucky and didn't fracture your jaw when your face hit the steering wheel, however when you were still unconscious, we stitched up several cuts on your face. Do you understand so far?'

Jenny blinked once to tell him that she understood, and Ian explained to the doctor the communication signals they had devised.

The doctor taped Jenny's ribs then said, 'Now that you're conscious, let me examine you and see how things are going.'

He asked Jenny to raise her arms one at a time, which she did very easily. Then he gently pulled the covers down past her feet. 'Now turn your right ankle. Now your left one.'

Jenny realised that she couldn't move her feet and her immediate panic showed in her hazel eyes and a tear slid down her cheek.

'Now, lift your right leg – now your left leg.'

Jenny couldn't comply, and she began openly weeping. Her parents were frozen in terrible fear for their daughter. They realised the serious implications of what they were seeing and hearing - that their daughter was paralysed, possibly for life.

'I'm going to use a device to check your nerve reactions. Did you feel that?' Dr. Warren asked as he ran a device over the bottom of her left foot. Jenny couldn't see what he was doing and was unable to feel anything at all. Then she couldn't feel anything when he did the same thing on her right foot.

She attempted to speak, but again couldn't open her mouth wide enough for anyone to understand what she was saying.

'I know you're frightened. But your paralysis could be temporary and may ease off when the swelling goes down around your spinal cord. In the meantime, we'll be placing you in traction. This means that you'll have weights put on your neck and feet to try to relieve the pressure on your vertebrae.'

Dr. Warren placed an order for the traction equipment. When it arrived, he explained what he was doing as he attached slings around each of her legs. These were held in place with wide tensor bandages that went from her ankles to her thighs. Slowly he added weights to the bottom of the two slings that hung over the bottom of her bed. Jenny would have been pulled downwards in the bed if the nurses on each side of her had not held her body in place.

'Now, I'm going to remove your cervical collar – please don't move your head at all when I do.' the doctor warned.

Dr. Warren then removed her cervical collar and placed a soft, but strong cotton device under her chin that had openings for her ears and ended at the top of her head. As he tucked in her hair he looked carefully at Jenny to ensure that she was still all right. She appeared to be fine, so he slowly attached weights to the hooks on each side of the traction device. This forced her head to stay parallel to the bed making the ceiling of her room the only thing she could see. She had no pillow, so she lay flat on the bed. She could feel the weights pulling at her from both directions. It was a very uncomfortable feeling, her ribs hurt as they were stretched and for a few minutes she panicked.

Dr. Warren stood beside her at the head of her bed so was able to gauge her response to the unfamiliar pressure. 'I know it feels uncomfortable, but you'll get used to it soon. It really is necessary to help ease the pressure on your spinal column.' he reassured Jenny as he patted her shoulder. 'I'll be back shortly to see how you're doing.'

When he returned fifteen minutes later Jenny still felt very uncomfortable and her head was pounding. Jenny winced with the pain and wondered how she was going to tell the doctor about her headache. She tried using body language and banged one of her fists into her other palm then pointed to her head. Dr. Warren realised from reading her body language that she had a terrible headache. 'Do you have a headache?' he asked.

Jenny blinked once.

'I'll order some pain relief for you. Now try to relax. I'm going to speak with your parents. See if you can get some rest.'

The nurse gave Jenny an injection and she drifted off to sleep. Dr. Warren ushered Ian and Martha out of the room, led them to a consulting room and gestured for them to enter. Her parents were aware of the gravity of the situation. They knew that he likely had some really bad news for them as he explained Jenny's condition. Ian reached over and held Martha's hand.

'How bad is she doctor?' Ian asked, full of concern about his daughter's sudden incapacitation.

'I'm not going to deceive you – there's only about a fifty-fifty chance that she will walk again. Right now she's paralysed from the waist down, so has no control over her bowel and bladder functions. She will have to wear adult diapers and we'll catheterise her. We'll keep her in traction until the swelling goes down and do periodic X-rays to determine whether the pressure in her spinal column has lessened.

'She should be able to talk better tomorrow when some of the swelling goes down around her mouth. We don't think she will be badly scarred from those injuries but will likely have one little scar on the left side of her bottom lip. She was very lucky the collision didn't break her jawbone when she hit the steering wheel. Several of her teeth have been loosened and she may lose some of them eventually. We've put stitches in the gash she has in her right knee, but there was no major damage to her knee. And as you saw, we've taped her ribs because of the two fractures. We've checked and there was no damage done to her lungs by the broken ribs. Do you have any questions?'

'How long will she be in the hospital?' Martha asked then mentally chastised herself for asking such an irrelevant question. She thought, 'Jenny's whole life is in turmoil and yet I wasted the doctor's valuable time by asking such a silly question.'

'That's hard to determine.' he replied. 'It depends on what happens with her spinal cord. We'll know much more by the end of next week.

'She's married, isn't she? Where's her husband?' Dr. Warren asked.

'He's in the Winnipeg General Hospital. He was admitted two days ago with viral pneumonia. He'll likely be in there until after the weekend. We'll let him know about Jenny's accident.'

Dr. Warren nodded his head and returned with them to Jenny's room. The pain medication had worked, and she was still asleep. 'She'll probably sleep for a couple of hours.' he said quietly. 'Why don't you go up to the hospital and explain her condition to her husband? If he wants, he can call me and discuss her treatment.' he added, as he gave them two of his business cards—one for them and one for Russ.

They nodded, and Ian said, 'We'll be back in a few hours.'

Chapter 3

When Jenny awoke from her sleep, Ian and Martha had returned with the supplies Jenny would need for her hospital stay.

'We've been up to see Russ, so he knows about your accident. He wanted to sign himself out of the hospital, but we convinced him not to do so. He is still far too weak to even consider that. We told him that we would keep him informed of your progress. He thinks they will let him leave the hospital on Monday, especially because of your accident.'

Ian told her that Russ had finally resigned himself to the fact that he would have to concentrate his efforts on getting better, so he would in turn be able to help Jenny.

After her parents left, Jenny couldn't help but wonder what was going to happen to her and how she would cope if she was permanently paralysed. Swimming would be impossible if she couldn't move her legs. More importantly, would Russ want to stay married to her now that she might not be able to walk? They'd only been married for six months and had no children, so he might not want to stay with her. She wished she could go back to that morning when she was fine and cursed the driver of the other car for the pain and suffering she was going through. She had no idea who was driving the other car.

The nurse arrived with her 'dinner' that was given intravenously. It was impossible for Jenny to open her mouth wide enough for even a straw. She wasn't very hungry anyway so was not disappointed because she couldn't eat. She did crave a good cup of tea, but realised that it would be some days before she could enjoy food or her favourite beverage.

The next day, she was able to leave the ICU ward and was taken to an orthopaedic ward on the fourth floor. As the attendant wheeled her bed into the room he introduced

Jenny to her roommate. 'Your roommate's name is Elaine Harrington. Elaine – this is Jenny.'

'Hi Jenny.'

As Jenny was being settled Elaine continued, 'I broke my ankle skiing and it's really a mess. They pinned it and put it in a cast. They say it will be months before I'll be able to walk properly.'

The attendant told Elaine about Jenny's difficulty in speaking until her mouth healed and explained the one for 'yes' and two for 'no' communication system. He also suggested that, because it would be difficult for them to communicate unless Elaine was standing beside her bed and Jenny being prone on the bed, that they change the communication system.

'Jenny, why don't you raise your right arm for 'yes,' and your left for 'no?'' he suggested.

'Sounds good to me.' Replied Elaine as Jenny raised her right hand.

They soon settled in for the night. Shortly after midnight, Jenny woke up to find herself all wrapped up in her traction device. Somehow, in her sleep, she'd turned over and now lay helplessly on her stomach. She knew she shouldn't be lying that way, especially with her head turned towards her right side. She tried to find the bell to call a nurse for help but couldn't find it. Thankfully, she remembered she had a roommate who could help her.

'Elaine,' she mumbled. There was no reply. 'Elaine,' she shouted again. It hurt tremendously to speak, but she needed to get help. Finally, Elaine sleepily replied, 'What's the matter Jenny?'

Jenny said, 'Nurse – bell.' Elaine looked over at Jenny and realised what had happened and immediately pushed her bell to call for help. A nurse arrived and advised Jenny that she was going to get help to turn her over. Two nurses and an orderly unhooked her traction device, carefully turned her over onto her back and re-attached the traction weights.

'How do you feel,' asked the nurse when Jenny was hooked up again in the right position. 'How is your neck? Does it hurt?'

'No.' Jenny signalled with by raising her left hand. Then she raised her eyebrows, shrugged her shoulders and put both hands out palm up.

'We've called Dr. Warren to see if there's anything else we should do to stabilise you.' the nurse responded.

The nurse returned a few minutes later and explained, 'Dr. Warren has ordered another X-ray series to see if there's been any damage done when you turned over.'

X-Rays were taken and processed. Jenny lay in her bed wide-eyed and fearful that she had caused more damage to her already fragile spinal column. An hour later, her nurse came back to Jenny's room, 'The X-ray technician has assured Dr. Warren that you have not caused further damage to your neck and back.' Then she added, 'I've got something that will stop it from happening again.'

She placed two rather large rubber wedges beside Jenny's head, so she could not inadvertently turn over in her sleep again. Jenny received another injection for the pain so she could sleep during what remained of that night.

The next morning, Jenny was terribly embarrassed when she smelled that she'd had a bowel movement during the night. She buzzed for the nurse who came and cleaned her up. It was then that Jenny realised she was wearing adult diapers. Her urine wasn't a problem because she was catheterised, but she needed the diapers in case she had a bowel movement. They had placed her on medication to keep her bowels from becoming constipated, but she could not feel when her body was releasing its contents. How embarrassed she felt – so helpless and dirty.

Shortly after, the nurse brought Jenny a large glass with a straw. 'This is your breakfast. It's high calorie and should keep you going till lunch. Now let's make sure your mouth isn't too sore to suck on the straw.'

Jenny tried drawing the food through the straw and was pleased that it didn't hurt too much. Because she needed to stay flat on her back, it was necessary for the nurse to stay with her while she drank the fluid in case she choked.

After breakfast when the nurse had gone, Elaine said, 'You sure did a good job of tying yourself up last night. You looked like a trussed-up turkey ready for basting.'

Jenny and Elaine got the giggles and Jenny ended up with tears running down her cheeks but not wholly from the funny idea, but because it hurt her ribs so much when she laughed.

'We make a great pair,' said Elaine. 'Shall I tell you about my skiing accident?'

Jenny raised her right hand.

'I've been skiing for several years and thought I knew my limitations. I was skiing along feeling like the Queen of the Mountain, showing off to my friends when suddenly I found myself airborne. I remember seeing the big tree looming up in front of me and taking a quick look around realised that I'd strayed off the main trail into the trees at the side of the run.

'I remember hitting the tree and having snow all over me, then I must have passed out. When I came to, I was in agony – my leg felt like it was in a bear trap. I waved my arms around and felt as if I was floating on air and wondered for a moment or two whether I was dead and had gone to either Heaven or Hell. My head felt as if it would burst. Then I felt something sliding along my back and felt a person's hands on me as they strapped me onto something solid. I looked over to see who was helping me, but I couldn't see a thing. The man must have noticed that I was conscious and said, 'Did you have a good flight?'

'Then I felt his hands sliding over my face, brushing off the snow, but I couldn't see anything except a dim light and what looked like grey clouds. Then he lifted up my ski goggles and I realised that I wasn't going blind – my goggles had been covered with snow. The next few minutes I did feel as if I had landed in Heaven. I looked into the most brilliant blue eyes on a handsome face that was to die for. He was gorgeous in his bright yellow ski patrol jacket!

'I asked him who he was, 'I'm a ski patroller and there are two other fellows below us helping.' he said as he continued to tighten straps around my body. I asked him what he was doing.

'You're hanging upside down in a tree. Your leg is caught in the branches of a tree and I'm quite sure your ankle is broken. Do you hurt anywhere else?' he asked.

'My head hurts, but I think that's because I am lying upside down and I know I was hit by quite a bit of snow when I landed on the tree.'

'As a precaution, I'm putting on a neck brace to secure your head' he said as he raised the rope with the brace attached to it and as he attached it, said, 'I'm strapping you to the rescue board, so we can lower you out of the tree and take you down the ski hill to the lodge.' he added as he placed my arms over my chest and tightened the chest straps over them.

'He had already tied the rescue board to the tree. Then he warned me that what he had to do next would be very painful. 'I'll be raising the rescue board, so I can ease your foot out of the tree, so I can place it on the board. That will likely hurt like hell, but it has to be done.'

'He didn't lie. I couldn't control the scream that came out of my mouth when he moved my leg. I think I passed out with the pain and by the time I came to he had secured my leg in splints and had fastened my legs to the board. Then I heard him shout to the two ski patrollers below us, 'I think she's ready to be lowered.'

'They slowly lowered me to the ground and soon 'Mr. Gorgeous' and another ski patroller were skiing with me and my rescue board down the hill. It didn't take very long for them to get me to the lodge. The other patroller had called ahead and there was an ambulance waiting for us there. Before I was transferred from the rescue board onto the ambulance gurney, I spoke to gorgeous, 'What's your name?'

'It's Tom McElroy.' he replied shyly.

'Will you come up to the hospital to visit me?' I boldly asked him.

'He said he would try. But he hasn't come yet and my accident happened three days ago. I'm devastated. I guess I'll have to wait till my ankle heals up and I can ski again. Even before then, I'll go back to the hill and hang around the ski lodge until I can see him again. He's a real hunk; is over six feet tall, broad shouldered and is an excellent skier. I sure hope I see him again.'

Jenny mumbled a reply in sympathy and dozed off for another sleep. Later when Dr. Warren visited, she asked for something to write on. One of the nurses gave her one, and she scrawled, 'Could you see if a dentist can come to examine my teeth?' Her teeth still ached terribly and she wanted to know what would happen to them. He promised to make arrangements for an oral surgeon to see her.

On Monday morning Dr. Bennet, examined her teeth and ordered dental X-rays. When they were developed, he explained his findings. 'When you smashed your mouth on the steering wheel, it damaged most of your front teeth. All twelve of your front teeth are cracked; six on top, six on the bottom. They'll likely break off as soon as you start eating solid food. The ones at the sides are so full of fillings that the only thing I can suggest to you so you don't have a lifetime of trouble is to extract all of them and wear dentures. Your four wisdom teeth haven't come through either and you wouldn't have had room for them in your small mouth anyway, so they will have to be removed as well.'

'Oh no!' she mumbled as she covered her mouth with her hands. It was as if she were trying to protect her already sore mouth against the horrible news the dental surgeon had given her.

'For sure, the twelve front teeth should be removed. An alternative would be to make partial plates to replace those teeth. If you decide to have that done, I can remove them with local freezing or put you under general anaesthetic. I think you probably should have general anaesthesia because your mouth is so bruised and sore already.'

'Can I think about this for a while and get back to you?' she wrote.

'I'll come back tomorrow to see what you decide. and we can commence with whatever treatment you choose.'

Jenny nodded. and he left the room. She thought long and hard about what she should do. When her parents visited that afternoon. Jenny was pleased to see that Russ was with them. He'd been discharged from the hospital that morning. She frowned as she noted that he still looked very weak and pale which was so different from his usual fit self.

Earlier in the day, a nurse had changed the bandages on her face. While they were off, Jenny asked for a mirror and looked at the stitches both inside and outside her mouth and wondered if she would be disfigured for life. As she gazed at her reflection her eyes widened as she observed her two black eyes and the black, blue and even green bruises on the rest of her face not covered by the bandages. She knew she looked a mess – as if someone had taken a baseball bat to her face.

Jenny was watching Russ's face as he entered the room and wondered what he would say or do when he saw her all trussed up in traction and saw the still-raw looking stitches around her mouth. She knew her lips were still very swollen. Although Ian and Martha had explained her injuries, Russ was shocked to see how seriously injured she was. The woman on the bed didn't even look like Jenny she was so disfigured from her facial injuries.

Russ just stared and said, 'You look very sore. Where can I kiss you where it won't hurt?'

Jenny pointed to her forehead. He gave a smacking kiss to that area, stood back and smiled sadly at her.

'What do your doctors say? Any good news?' he asked.

Jenny had prepared for this question and earlier had written a note explaining what she'd learned from the oral surgeon. She handed this note to Russ:

'I spoke with an oral surgeon this morning. He has bad news. Twelve of my front teeth will have to be removed – six on the top – six on the bottom. They're cracked and will likely break off when I'm able to eat solid food. And the others are so full of fillings that he's suggested that they too be removed and replaced with full dentures. He will have to dig for and remove my wisdom teeth as well. The only other alternative is for me to get two partials – one for the top six teeth and another for the bottom ones. However, he did mention that the teeth that would be used as anchors for the plates were not in the best condition and could cause problems later.'

'What have you decided to do?' Russ asked.

'I don't really know what to do. What would you do if you had to make this decision?' she wrote awkwardly as she looked from Russ to her parents.

The four of them discussed her options and left it up to Jenny to decide what she would do. Genetically Jenny knew she came from a family that had notoriously bad teeth. Her parents had worn dentures since they were in their mid-thirties, so she knew that sooner or later she probably would end up with dentures.

Ian, Martha and Russ watched as she wrote awkwardly on the writing tablet. It was hard to do because she had to remain flat on her back and the tablet kept flopping down onto her face.

'I've decided to have the oral surgeon remove them all while I'm in the hospital and fit me for dentures. That way, I should have them by the time I leave the hospital. He will be seeing me again tomorrow and will proceed with the removal as soon as an operating room is available.'

'You poor kid,' her father commiserated as he gave her a kiss on her forehead. 'You've been through so much already – I hate the fact that you'll be facing more pain and suffering.'

'I'll be fine Dad. You know how tough I am.' she wrote. In truth, Jenny was scared again that Russ wouldn't want her. First. she might not walk again, and now she would be like an old woman with false teeth.

They visited for a while, then Ian and Martha drove Russ home. Jenny promised she would have someone phone them after she had communicated with the oral surgeon.

The next day, although she was still hooked up to the traction device, the nurse was able to raise her bed a few inches. so she felt less isolated. Jenny was finally able to see around her room a bit better and was able to do more things for herself.

That afternoon when the oral surgeon visited, Jenny gave him her decision.

He replied, 'I've already checked. and I can do the procedure tomorrow.'

'Good. We might as well get it over with.' she wrote.
Elaine was getting around on crutches now and was able to sit at Jenny's bedside. They had been looking at the clothing the movie stars were wearing in a magazine when Elaine looked up and gave a little squeal.

In the door came what Jenny knew had to be Elaine's 'Mr. Gorgeous.' He smiled at Elaine and handed her a small bouquet of flowers. Elaine introduced him to Jenny and they decided to have a cup of coffee at the cafeteria. Jenny mentally agreed with Elaine – Tom was gorgeous and seemed to like Elaine. When Elaine returned to the room after Tom had gone, she was in seventh heaven and made a dangerous one-legged twirl on her crutches.

'He says he'll come up to see me again and asked whether he could take me out to dinner when I'm out of the hospital! Isn't he gorgeous?' she crowed.

Jenny raised her right arm up high and pumped it back and forth giving her agreement.

That night Jenny couldn't have anything to eat or drink after midnight. At seven the next morning before her surgery, a nurse gave Jenny an injection. 'This will relax you. In a few minutes we'll wheel you down to the operating theatre. Normally you would sit in a dentist chair to remove your teeth, but because you're in traction, we'll be leaving you in your own bed during the procedure.'

Soon Jenny was wheeled into the operating theatre. She was very groggy and didn't even notice when they removed the traction devices and the anaesthesiologist slipped the anaesthetic into the cannula the nurse had already inserted above her wrist before she left her room.

Her parents and Russ were waiting for her when she returned from the recovery room. Jenny's mouth felt very raw and she was reluctant to talk without teeth. She was very embarrassed, but her parents assured her that she didn't look much different than when her mouth had been so swollen from the sutures.

Day by day, the swelling went down on her many bruises and Jenny was able to talk more normally. She could now eat soft foods like Jell-O and ice cream but would not be offered solid food until her mouth and gums were healed.

Several days later the oral surgeon took impressions of her gums, so he could prepare a set of temporary dentures for her. When he placed them into her sore mouth, he said to her, 'These dentures will do until the swelling has completely gone down, then we will do permanent ones. How do they feel?'

'As if I have a mouth full of marbles,' she mumbled as she tried to get used to the feeling of having something so foreign in her mouth.

That day, she was finally able to eat soft foods. It hurt like hell to eat, but she stuck with it. Then her nurse showed her how to remove her dentures and how to clean them so there would be no food stuck under the dentures to irritate her still very raw tooth sockets.

Jenny and Elaine became close friends. Soon Jenny could speak rather than write so they had many conversations about their childhoods and family life. Jenny was sad when she learned Elaine was going to be discharged from the hospital. They swapped phone numbers and promised to get together after they were both able to get around again.

Every day Dr. Warren checked her reflexes. Jenny knew that she still didn't have any feeling in her legs. When she was alone, she prodded her abdomen to try to determine where her paralysis began. It was just below her belly button that she lost sensation.

Something Missing

Chapter 4

Ten days after his wife's accident and a week after his own release from hospital, Russ was well enough to go back to work. Because he was working the four-to-twelve evening shift at the railway, he chose to visit Jenny on his way to work. To give them private time together, Jenny's parents and friends usually came to the hospital to see her in the evening or in the early afternoon before Russ was expected to arrive on his way to work.

Two weeks after her accident, Dr. Warren examined Jenny and said, 'I've decided to disconnect the traction. It doesn't seem to have improved your injuries, and I'm sure it's very uncomfortable for you to have it on all the time. However, you'll still have to wear a cervical collar for several months.'

He rolled up her bed to a sitting position and for the first time Jenny was able to observe her hospital room and see those walking down the corridor outside her door.

'Yes, it will be good to get rid of the traction. It's about time I got up from this bed and started living again!'

'This afternoon after you get used to doing without the traction, I'll ask the nurse to put you in a wheelchair, so you can get up and around a bit.' he said as he smiled at her.

He noticed that she was looking so much better now that the swelling and bruising on her face had gone down. The scars around her mouth were small and didn't look as if they would detract from her beauty. She was still getting used to having 'a mouth full of marbles,' but she seemed to manage speaking and eating much better now.

That afternoon a nurse helped her into a wheelchair and gave her a tour of the ward. Then she showed Jenny how to set and remove the brake on her chair and gave her a set of gloves that would assist her to move the chair. 'From now on you will be able to do this by yourself. But you must ask us to help you move from your bed to the chair – then you'll be on your own.'

Two days later, a nurse from the rehabilitation section arrived. 'Hi. Jenny. I'm Angie Walker. I've got a bathing suit for you. You're a size twelve, aren't you?'

'Yes I am. What's the bathing suit for?

'I'm going to take you down for a swim.' she announced.

Angie helped her change into the bathing suit and replaced her cervical collar with a plastic one, so it could be worn in the pool. 'I'll take you into our rehabilitation pool to see if the buoyancy of the water will help you move your legs.'

At the pool, Angie helped Jenny shift into a special wheel chair that could be taken into the pool. She had already taken off her smock and Jenny saw that Angie too wore a bathing suit. Angie released the brake and rolled Jenny's wheelchair down the ramp and into the heated pool. Initially, knowing how helpless she was, Jenny was frightened, but bit by bit she was able to relax. Angie gently helped her to float out of the chair, carefully supporting her back and neck. The warm water felt so good on her skin after lying in a bed trussed up for so long. Jenny loved the water and had always been a good swimmer. Being in a pool again, made her remember the time in her life when swimming had been tremendously important to her.

She was eight years old and was climbing out of a local swimming pool, when an elderly man approached her and began talking to her. Immediately Jenny felt apprehensive as she recalled her mother's warning about men who seemed to be too friendly. But this older man had a kind face. He said, 'You're a good swimmer. Would you give my card to your parents and ask them to phone me?'

She nodded and accepted the card. As she tucked his card into a pocket of her swimming bag she wondered, 'What did the old man want?' He didn't linger but did a shallow dive into the water.

She completely forgot about his card until several days later when she noticed it sticking out of her swimming bag. 'Should I give it to my parents?' she pondered. Then curiosity got the better of her. After all, she'd just turned eight and was curious about everything.

'Mom, when I was swimming at the pool on Sunday, an old man came up to me and gave me this card. He asked me to give it to you because he wanted you to phone him. I don't know what he wants but he seemed like a nice man.'

'I'll call him to see what he has to say,' Martha replied. When her mother hung up the phone she said, 'I need to talk to your father, then I'll explain what the phone call was about.'

'I wonder what I've done?' Jenny wondered. 'I don't think I did anything wrong at the pool. I don't dunk other children and I did help that little girl with her swimming stroke.'

When her parents returned to the kitchen, Ian explained what they'd discussed. 'The man's name is 'Pop Wilson,' he said. 'He's our city's Olympic swimming coach. He wants to know if we will allow you to join his swim team. He thinks you have the potential to do very well. However, the lessons will be quite expensive, and we don't want to spend that kind of money unless you're really serious about training.'

He saw that Jenny was about to speak and held up his hand. Just six months before, Jenny'd had one communicable disease after another ending with whooping cough, so he was concerned about her health. Jenny was a small child with small bones and he wondered if her health would suffer.

'We know you love the water, but whether you'll have the dedication and stamina for the gruelling training schedule concerns us. You would have to train for two hours, three nights a week at the YWCA pool downtown. You would have to go by bus right from school, spring, autumn and winter and will be expected to practice extra on the weekends. What do you think? Do you want to do it?'

'Do I want to do it?' she'd exclaimed, 'Of course I do – you know how much I love the water. Please, please, can I join the swim club?' she said as she jumped up and down with excitement.

Jenny was crazy about water and swam whenever possible. For as long as she could remember, right after the last day of school, her family would board a train to Grand Beach where they rented a small cabin for the summer. Grand Beach was a magical childhood place. It had fine white silicone sand, huge sand dunes and quite often there were large waves to play in. She and her friends spent most of their days either jumping over the rocks along the side of the lake or swimming in the water. It was great fun.

Grand Beach provided wonderful, happy, summer memories. She remembered the huge dance pavilion that she could only enter when she was with her parents. Families and all age groups enjoyed the music of the band that was hired by the railway for the summer season. Jenny remembered watching her mother and father as they paid their dime for a ticket and went on the dance floor to dance up a storm.

She remembered the boardwalk that extended from the train station to the lagoon along the beachfront. It was hot and crowded during the day, but when it was lit up at night it was a magical place. The wooden boardwalk provided sure footing for shoe-clad feet but could be treacherous for bare feet with many a sliver being pulled from feet that dared to walk on it without shoes. Under the boardwalk the shade was welcome. Treasure hunters could be rewarded with some loose change and itinerant travellers found the boardwalk an ideal overnight shelter.

The hot dog and soft drink stands were Jenny's favourites, but the carousel was as well. It was an awesome and magical structure, filled with hand-crafted animals: studs, mares and ponies, whirling in an endless circle to the tinkling music, their manes flying, teeth bared, hooves raised, forever frozen in time.

Even after summer was over and her family returned to the city, Jenny was at the local pool swimming her heart out. She was so excited about this training possibility that she thought she would die if they didn't let her do it.

Her mother said, 'I'll tell you what. We'll pay for one year and then we'll see what happens after that.'

Jenny was determined not to let them down and seriously began her training. It was as gruelling as she'd been told it would be. Having to come out into twenty degree below zero temperature in winter after a swimming practice, would wear anyone down. After training sessions, she would take the long bus ride home, gobble something to eat and literally fall into bed, exhausted.

Her best swimming stroke was front crawl. Within a year she could swim over a hundred lengths of the pool with ease and began entering and winning most of her races. From then on, her parents decided that she was serious about her training, so they continued to enrol her in swim classes every year.

When Jenny was fourteen, six years after she'd started her training, Pop Wilson met with Ian and Martha. 'Jenny is ready for national and international competitions and I think we'd better prepare for that.' he said.

'What will that involve?' Ian asked. He knew that with their limited budget they couldn't afford to pay too much.

'Jenny and her chaperone would have to travel to swim meets in other provinces. Then if she won them, she'd be ready to compete internationally.' he replied.

'That will cost quite a bit won't it?' Martha said, wringing her hands.

'Yes. Unfortunately, it will. Sponsors in Canada are more likely to fund ice hockey or figure skating – not swimming. So, you'd be on your own for the cost of the travel and competition fees.'

'I have a small child at home. I can't travel with Jenny.' lamented her mother. Jenny's sister Susan was only four. 'Don't they have a chaperone that could be responsible for several children?'

'We really encourage a parent or relative to come with the child, especially when they're under-age like Jenny.'

'Let's discuss this and we'll get back to you.' said Ian.

That night Jenny, Ian and Martha had a long discussion. It soon became clear that her family would suffer financially if she continued to compete past this stage of training.

'Honey, we'd do anything to help,' said Martha, 'but we don't want to use the money we've put aside for your brother's, your sister's and your education. We'll need quite a bit of it soon to send your bother to university.' Her brother Jeff was a whiz at school and since he was very young he'd decided that he wanted to go to university and obtain a chartered accountancy degree.

'Mom, it sounds like we can't afford this,' Jenny said as she wiped a tear off her cheek. 'I don't want my family to suffer because of my dream. I think I should drop out of competition and give my space to someone who can afford the training.'

So Jenny had dropped out of swimming. However, her six years of intensive training were not a waste of time as she was to learn after her car accident. Pop Wilson had taught her three very important lessons. The first was to take the word 'failure' out of her vocabulary – that if she had tried her best but hadn't succeeded – that's all that had happened – she had not succeeded. Not that she had failed, but that she had not succeeded.

His second lesson was to teach his swimmers how to go past the wall – that invisible wall, that often stopped good athletes from being top athletes. The best athletes found something within themselves that kept them striving to win long after most had stopped trying.

The third big benefit was that when she grew up she had an extremely high bone density that had obviously helped her during her car accident.

Chapter 5

During her first session in the hospital rehabilitation pool Jenny realised that the water did not seem to help her to move her legs. They just hung there, knees bent and they would have pulled her to the bottom of the pool if Alice hadn't supported her. However, every morning, she continued with her water therapy.

One morning, Dr. Warren visited her room as usual. He had a terribly sad look on his face. It was obvious that he had bad news for Jenny. 'We've done more tests and X-rays, and I'm sorry to tell you that you are permanently paralysed from the waist down and won't walk again. We'll be discharging you the day after tomorrow.'

Jenny cried and cried. When she had finished sobbing, she asked the nurse for a phone and talked to both Russ and her parents. They all suggested that she ask for a second opinion. The next morning, Jenny asked Dr. Warren if he would arrange to have another orthopaedic specialist see her before she left the hospital.

'It's not that I don't believe you, but I need a second opinion.' she said shyly.

'I understand completely. I'd do the same. Let me make the arrangements.' he replied.

The other specialist went over all the test results and examined Jenny. He looked at Jenny and just shook his head confirming her worst fears.

'I'm sorry I can't give you any good news. I'm afraid I have to confirm Dr. Warren's diagnosis.'

'Will I be having any further treatment or physiotherapy?' she asked.

'No, we don't think physiotherapy will make any difference to your ability to walk again.' he replied.

After the two specialists had left her hospital room Jenny realised that she was furious; furious at the other driver; furious at having lost her teeth; furious about not being able to walk and furious about life in general. She placed a pillow over her abdomen and pounded it repeatedly. She felt so defeated and depressed that she didn't want to go on living.

'What did I ever do to deserve this?' she wailed. She cried for a long time. Then her fighting spirit kicked in and she mentally prepared for her next battle.

That afternoon, before she was released from hospital, Dr. Warren explained that he'd arranged for a carer to be with her to help her manage at home.

Russ drove her to their home. He'd made several changes to their home so that Jenny to manage easier. They were home only a short time when the doorbell rang. It was her carer, who introduced herself, 'Hi, I'm Janet Blakely.'

They shook hands then Janet explained what would happen. 'I'll come in the afternoon just before Russ leaves for work and will stay until he returns shortly after midnight. I know he's off Wednesday and Thursday, so I won't come those days. I'll do this for two weeks and the third week will come only Friday, Sunday and Tuesday. After that you'll be on your own.'

She noticed Jenny's look of panic and quickly added, 'But you can call me any time after that if you need further help.'

Janet taught Russ and Jenny how to get her into and out of bed and into her wheel chair. Soon Jenny was able to accomplish these tasks without assistance using the bar that had been installed over her bed. Janet also showed Jenny how to move herself out of her wheelchair into and out of a chair that was set up in her shower. 'It's very important that you remember to put the brake on your wheelchair, so it doesn't roll away from you when you are transferring to and from it.'

Then she explained to Russ the importance of moving things down to lower cupboards, so Jenny could reach the items she required to perform her everyday tasks and activities.

At first, Jenny had problems propelling herself around in her wheel chair, and her arms and shoulders ached from the effort. She had not developed the muscular shoulders and arms that modern swimmers have because her training had not included weight lifting. But soon Jenny was able to do most of the things she had to do for herself without Janet or Russ's assistance.

After Russ left for work on her first day alone, Jenny felt a bit of panic wondering whether she could cope by herself. She sat in her wheelchair looking around her empty home feeling very frightened and alone. To help her cope, she decided to phone Elaine and see how she was doing. Elaine heard the panic in Jenny's voice.

'Would you like me to come over?' she asked. She was able to drive even though her left foot was still in an ankle cast.

'That would be great!' exclaimed Jenny, so pleased that she wouldn't have to spend the evening alone.

Elaine was very glad to hear from Jenny. They had a wonderful evening laughing over silly things. Elaine was now dating Tom, and they were really enjoying each other's company. At the end of the evening when Elaine had gone home, Jenny realised that it was the first time she'd felt happy since before her accident. Elaine was also pleased that she had come and vowed to do so regularly in the future. She and Jenny kept in touch, called each other at least once a week and Elaine drove over to visit Jenny many evenings when Russ was at work.

After helping Jenny for three weeks, Janet said, 'This is my last day with you. However, if you find you need more help here's the number you can call for assistance.' She gave Jenny a hug and they said goodbye.

Jenny found it quite intimidating being on her own at first. However, her parents had spoken with Jenny's next-door neighbour Agnes Evans who agreed to be on call should Jenny need anything or if she felt unwell. Agnes also helped by stopping by to see if there were any groceries or supplies Jenny might need.

Jenny, always an avid reader, found she now had time to read as much as she wanted to. She read novels, magazines and the daily newspapers. The second evening when she was on her own, she was reading the newspaper when she spotted an interesting article. As she read it, she became more and more excited. It was all about a new revolutionary medical breakthrough called biofeedback. The article explained that physical therapists used biofeedback to help stroke victims regain movement in paralysed muscles.

'I wonder if they could help me?' she wondered as she continued to read the article. It went on, 'Psychologists use it to help tense and anxious clients learn to relax. Specialists in many different fields use biofeedback to help their patients cope with pain.'

Jenny realised that biofeedback might help her regain movement in her paralysed muscles. She excitedly read through the remainder of the information about biofeedback.

'Biofeedback operates on the notion that we have the innate ability and potential to influence the automatic functions of our bodies through the exertion of will and mind. Biofeedback has recently been shown to give us what had previously seemed an impossible degree of control over a variety of physiologic events.

'Biofeedback is based on the idea, confirmed by scientific studies, that people have the innate potential to influence with their minds many of the automatic, involuntary functions of their bodies. To help patients develop this ability, a biofeedback specialist uses signals from special monitoring equipment to teach patients how to control certain body functions and their responses, such as: brain activity, blood pressure, muscle tension, heart rate, skin temperature and sweat gland activity.

'You can receive biofeedback training in physical therapy clinics, medical centres and hospitals. A growing number of feedback devices and programs are being marketed for home use as well. But working with a therapist, initially, may provide the best long-term results.

Preparation depends on the type of biofeedback therapy used. A typical biofeedback session lasts thirty to sixty minutes. The length and number of sessions will be determined by your condition and how quickly you learn to control your physical responses.

'During a biofeedback session, a therapist will apply electrical sensors to different parts of your body. These sensors will monitor your body's physiological response to stress — for instance, your muscle contraction during a tension headache — then feed the information back to you via cues such as a beeping sound or a flashing light. The feedback will allow you to begin to associate your body's response — in this case, headache pain — with certain physical functions, such as your muscles tensing.

'Once you begin to recognise that your headache is a result of tense muscles, the next step is to learn how to invoke positive physical changes in your body, such as relaxing those specific muscles, when your body is physically or mentally stressed. Your eventual goal will be to produce these responses on your own, outside the therapist's office and without the help of technology.

'Experts aren't entirely sure how the biofeedback therapy works. Many people who've tried it can't explain how they're able to control their bodies, yet experience improvement in their symptoms.'

Jenny was so excited she could hardly restrain herself. 'I must look into this,' she thought. The next morning while Russ was out buying groceries, she phoned the hospital she'd been in just three weeks before.

'Hello, I'm Jenny Carponi. I was a patient in your hospital until three weeks ago. Can you tell me whether you have a biofeedback specialist on your staff?'

'Sorry we don't, but we have a list of them we can give you and you can choose one you think might be helpful. Now let me see … where did I put that list? Ah – here it is.'

The receptionist gave Jenny a list of three specialists she might want to call. Jenny jotted down the three specialists' phone numbers and addresses and decided that the one nearest her home would probably be the best one. When she called to make an appointment, they were able to fit her in the next morning. The day of the appointment, she told Russ she had an appointment at another specialist's office but didn't let him know that her orthopaedic specialist hadn't referred her to him. He left her at the office while he did an errand saying he would be back in an hour to get her.

How enlightening was her visit and how uplifted she felt after that first appointment! Dr. Bowles hooked her up to a machine and showed her how it worked, and how she could eventually be able to use the techniques herself without the need to be hooked up to the machine. After their session and Jenny was back in the waiting room waiting for Russ, she knew she had to stem her excitement, so Russ wouldn't know what she was up to.

She had several sessions that week and was hopeful that biofeedback would work for her. However, she didn't want Russ or her parents and get their hopes up that she could walk again, so she didn't tell them about this special treatment.

When she was alone, she practiced biofeedback at least four or five times a day concentrating mainly on moving her feet. She realised she'd have to push herself really hard and *go past the wall* if she wanted to walk again. And she was going to walk again, if she died trying!

In addition to the biofeedback sessions, Jenny devised a way to drape a towel under her feet so that she could lift them up one at a time to exercise them. She asked Russ to help her but he always seemed to find some excuse not to help so she began to have doubts whether he still loved her or wanted her to improve.

Her parents had offered to help but she felt so guilty taking advantage of them when Russ was the one who should be helping her. After all he was her husband and it shouldn't be left to them to drop everything, so they could help her. However, because she wanted to walk so badly, she reluctantly resorted to asking them and even her neighbour Agnes Evans to assist with her physiotherapy. They helped by raising and lowering her legs and by making her legs move as if she were riding a bicycle. Her mother also became very adept at massaging her legs and back to relieve the muscle spasms Jenny often suffered after exercising.

Chapter 6

Jenny knew that when she was better she'd have to face a court case against the driver that had caused her accident. She and her family had learned that when the police investigated the accident site, they were able to determine that the vehicle that hit Jenny's car was travelling well over the speed limit even for bare concrete and was being driven far too fast for the treacherous road conditions. They also noted that even though Jenny had her foot solidly on the brake, her car had been pushed backwards for seventy-five feet.

Three months after her accident, when Jenny was sufficiently healed to testify against the driver, she and her grandmother attended a court hearing. After hearing their testimony, the judge charged the eighteen-year-old driver of the other car with reckless driving. He was given a heavy fine, ordered to pay Jenny's legal fees and his insurance company had to pay for all Jenny's medical expenses now and in the future.

As Jenny sat in the courtroom in her wheel chair, she, Russ, her parents and grandmother were shocked when they heard the judge give the amount of her compensation settlement for her pain and suffering.

'I award to the plaintiff, four thousand dollars as compensation for her pain and suffering.' he announced.

As Jenny sat in the courtroom in her wheel chair, she, Russ and her parents were highly insulted that the judge thought that her injuries and not being able to walk again warranted a settlement of a paltry four thousand dollars. How insulting. They stared unbelievingly at each other and Jenny's lawyer had to restrain Ian from standing up and shouting at the judge. They sat there shaking their heads.

'Court adjourned.' announced the court clerk.

In the hallway outside the court room, Jenny's lawyer explained that because she was employed as a secretary, her injuries would not receive the same settlement as would be awarded to those working in higher-paid positions.

'Can't we appeal?' Ian asked.

'You could, but you would be responsible for all legal and court costs – and you might not win.' was his sad advice.

Jenny, having no other real option, took the money, opened a bank account and put it into a high interest-bearing account in her name. She didn't want to put it into their joint account because she was still concerned that Russ might possibly walk out on her. If her marriage ended, she wanted to have at least this money to fall back on.

Chapter 7

Once when Jenny was practicing her biofeedback, she became aware that Russ was standing in the doorway observing her. 'What are you doing?' he asked, 'You're grunting and groaning as if you're working hard.'

'I'm using biofeedback to try and help with the muscle spasms I have in my back and legs.' she lied.

For six months, Jenny didn't give up even though she did not see or feel any response from the muscles she was trying to move. Her legs were now rather scrawny looking, even though she tried to keep them moving. From time to time she did feel very depressed and was ready to give up, but immediately she gave herself a mental kick in the pants and started practicing again. She was not going to give up!

Soon it was June, six months after her accident. Summer had arrived. and she was enjoying the sunshine, sitting in a lounge chair in their back yard. Russ was puttering with his car in the garage. so she knew he could not see her as she strained to move her muscles. That morning she concentrated on trying to move the toes on her left foot. As she watched her big toe – she thought she saw it move. 'Nah. That's just wishful thinking.' she told herself and tried it again. Again. it moved – up and down as she concentrated on it.

Jenny was ecstatic. She'd done it! She screamed for Russ, 'Russ come here quick!'

He rushed out from the garage wiping his oily hands on a rag, thinking she had fallen or been hurt somehow and was relieved to see her still sitting where he had left her. He did notice that her face was full of smiles and that she was terribly excited about something. 'What happened?' he asked.

'Watch!' she said as she pointed excitedly at her left foot.

Russ watched, wondering what she was doing. Then he too saw her toe move and looked incredulously at her. 'How did that happen?' he asked in awe.

'I've been practicing biofeedback for almost six months now. It's finally working! Please help me get inside so I can phone Mom and Dad and give them the good news.'

Her parents were beaming when they came to see what she had accomplished. After that breakthrough, Jenny insisted that she receive formal physiotherapy.

When she saw Dr Warren, he was amazed at her progress. He agreed with her and immediately arranged treatment at a local rehabilitation centre where she could receive ongoing treatment as an outpatient. He sent a letter to the other driver's insurance company that her recovery was still in progress and they were still responsible for these additional medical expenses.

Jenny couldn't understand why, but she went into a deep depression. She kept telling herself that she was on the road to recovery – that she had survived a terrible injury and was going to recover. Russ couldn't understand her behaviour and started withdrawing from her again. Her depression continued, until in desperation, she decided to talk to the minister of her church, Reverend Thompson. She asked him why she wasn't more elated over her progress. He explained that he thought she was suffering from Post Traumatic Stress Disorder (PTSD) – that she had been under tremendous pressure while she was incapacitated but wouldn't allow herself to wallow in it. Now that she was on the road to recovery, she was able to relax, and the immensity of her condition finally hit home in her subconscious.

Reverend Thompson explained that her Post Traumatic Stress Disorder was a natural emotional reaction to a deeply shocking and disturbing experience. Jenny had spent the past six months denying that anything traumatic had happened to her. Instead she had concentrated on making her legs move – against all odds. When they did move, she was boomeranged back to the first day she arrived in the hospital and realised that she would never walk again.

He added that post traumatic stress following an accident was largely due to the shattering of basic assumptions victims hold about themselves and the world, that the world is kind, caring, compassionate, generous, and giving; and the world is meaningful. He explained that there is growing recognition that PTSD can result from many types of shocking experiences including those who have been involved in traumatic road and plane accidents. He added that sometimes those who are in accidents may think that they are going mad. They are not, as PTSD is an injury, not an illness. Jenny left their session feeling revitalised and back on track now that she understood what was happening to her emotionally.

Suddenly she was energised and again spent more and more hours pushing herself to the limits of her endurance. The physiotherapist often placed Jenny in a heated pool and soon Jenny was swimming on her own with a flotation device around her tummy. Bit by bit she regained the use of first her feet, then her legs. It was a day for celebration when she was finally able to stand and hold her weight.

She was overwhelmed with joy at her progress. However, her gain in movement came with a serious drawback. Her legs and back now had feeling in them and she suffered from intense pain. She used biofeedback to try to relieve the pain but was only marginally successful. One morning her pain was so severe she called Dr. Warren to make an appointment to see if he could suggest a remedy. When she learned that he was on holidays and she'd have to wait four weeks for an appointment, she knew she had to do something drastic. She couldn't tolerate the intense pain any longer without relief. In desperation, she called a chiropractor, Dr. Redwood whom Elaine had recommended.

Jenny was apprehensive and wondered if she was doing the right thing, but after her first treatment that afternoon, she was amazed to learn that her pain was greatly relieved. Her pain had lessened to such a degree that it was as if someone had removed an opaque piece of plastic from in front of her eyes. She felt wonderful and almost pain free for the first time in months.

Her excitement lasted until she got up the next morning and she was again in intense pain. Luckily, she had another appointment with Dr. Redwood that day. When she saw him he explained, 'Everything along your spine has been such a mess for so long, that it will take months of treatment to encourage your back to stay in place for any length of time. Are you willing to keep coming until we're able to stabilise it?'

'Oh yes! Yesterday was wonderful after you put everything in place again. I'll do anything to get it to stay that way permanently.'

Dr. Redwood also recommended that she receive regular massages in addition to her physiotherapy sessions, so her muscles would remain relaxed instead of in spasm. She asked him to send a letter to the insurance company telling them of this additional treatment that had been recommended.

So, Jenny received regular treatment with Dr. Redwood and had a sports massage every two weeks. Soon she was able to go for longer and longer periods of time between visits. Throughout the years, she still had to make occasional visits for treatment, but in some years she had only one or two treatments. She was able to do everything she'd done before her accident, but knew if she fell the wrong way, she could be paralysed again. So, she knew that horseback riding, downhill skiing and participating in swinging sports such as badminton, golf and tennis were out of the question. Other than that, her life returned to normal.

It was after Jenny had completely recovered from her accident that she looked seriously at the life she shared with Russ. She realised that all was not going well in their relationship and knew she would have to do something to get their relationship back on track. Jenny craved adult conversation and with Russ on a four-to-twelve shift with Wednesdays and Thursdays off, she spent five evenings alone and two of those evenings were over the weekend when all her friends were out socialising.

Chapter 8

All Jenny wanted to do when she grew up was to get married and have children. Even thought her parents had offered to pay for a university education, having a career wasn't in her plans. She wanted a marriage – one just like her parents had where the gender boundaries were blurred, and everyone pitched in when there was a job to do. Her man would call his wife 'Hon' and would never fail to give his wife a kiss when he left home and when he returned. That's what her father did. His wasn't a long-drawn out kiss, but a loving peck on the cheek and a pat on his wife's shoulder to show her he loved her.

Both her parents set a good example for their three children. Their first child, a son they named Jeff, was born with a club foot the year after their marriage. Jenny arrived fifteen months later in 1939, one week before World War II started and their unexpected baby Susan arrived in 1949 when Jenny was ten.

Jenny's mother, Martha and her grandparents had been born in Canada, but her great-grandparents had been born in Ireland. Jenny often wondered whether her mother's life would have been different if the tradition of her day hadn't discouraged women from working after marriage. Before her marriage Martha had worked at Eaton's Department Store in their catalogue sales department. She excelled at mathematics, so Jenny believed she would have made an excellent accountant. Her large vocabulary was gleaned from pouring over crossword puzzles most of her life. However, her mother seemed to enjoy staying at home with her children – keeping herself busy doing volunteer work for the Red Cross or preparing bandages for the Cancer Institute when the children were in school. She was the first to volunteer to look after sick relatives or visit them in the hospital.

Jenny's father, Ian, had been seventeen when he emigrated from Scotland, but had worked hard since he was thirteen. Ian came from a rather large family that had been raised mainly by his mother. The oldest in his family was Jack, then Joan, Jane, Ian, Mark and George. Ian's father and one brother had died of diphtheria when he was only six. The family worked hard to be able to pay for their passages and immigrate to Canada. The children contributed to buying their mother's ticket and after several years they all settled in or around Winnipeg, in the centre of Canada. His close-knit family continued their strong work ethic and remained close throughout their lives. Their families continued the tradition that if a chore required doing in a home, everyone pitched in – no gender boundaries.

Ian worked hard all his life and passed on his work ethic to his children who learned that 'You don't get what you don't work for.' When World War II started, Ian Harper was employed as a police constable with the City of Winnipeg Police Force. Even though he was thirty-five and would not likely have been called up to serve in the armed forces right away, he volunteered to go to war in early 1942. He was stationed in Britain and because of his police background, was posted to the Provost Corps and rode a motorcycle.

Jenny had only been three when Ian left for England and had no idea who he was when he returned to Canada in 1945. But it didn't take long for Jenny to adore her father because he always made her feel important and encouraged her with praise and support. After the war, Ian made the decision that he didn't want to be a police officer all his life. At the age of forty, while still working full-time as a railway police officer, he enrolled in courses that would qualify him as a stationary engineer. His older brother, Jack had already qualified and encouraged Ian to do the same. After two years of agonisingly hard study, he passed his exams and took a position as the stationery engineer at a veteran's hospital near their home in St. James, a suburb of

Winnipeg. Jenny always hoped that she would find a man like her father when she married.

Jenny's brother Jeff had a difficult time as a baby and young child. She remembered when he was about six years old hearing him grunting as he tried to turn over in the bunk bed below her. It was very difficult for him to do so because the shoes on his feet had been attached to a board that forced them to point outwards. Jeff had been born with a club foot and had suffered through three operations already. The boots were to encourage his left foot to slant slightly outwards as his right one did normally. To accomplish this, he had to wear the cumbersome device while he slept.

He'd ripped many sheets before his parents realised that if he wore long heavy socks under the shoes attached to the board, his feet could be left out of the sheet and blankets that covered the remainder of his body. This enabled him to turn over in his sleep. Because Martha had a knitting machine that she used to make socks for the soldiers during the war, she was able to make as many socks as Jeff required. However, it was still impossible for him to sleep on his side.

Jenny was only five but slept on the top bunk bed in their bedroom. It was simply impossible for Jeff to manage the ladder to the upper level and the room was too small to have the beds side-by-side. Because he couldn't get up during the night if he needed to go to the bathroom, it was Jenny's responsibility to wake one of their parents, so they could help him. To accomplish this, Jeff pulled on a cord that rang a little bell next to Jenny's pillow.

Jeff couldn't take part in any sports until his leg was fully healed, but he hoped that this would be the last of his suffering. He was stoic about his situation and found other things besides sports to occupy his time. He became so good at cards that he often beat his parents and friends. He had a mathematical mind and excelled in math at school, so much that he was advanced a year because of his proficiency.

Life hadn't been kind to Jeff. Ian had explained why the calf of what he called his 'bad leg,' was so scarred. When he was just two, he'd been put in a leg and foot cast after an operation. That night he screamed and screamed. When he was still screaming at midnight, he parents knew something was terribly wrong. It was Saturday night and their doctor's office was closed, so they bundled him off to the emergency ward. The doctors could see the agony Jeff was in and immediately removed the cast. As he removed it, some of the skin from Jeff's calf came with it. Someone in the operating room had put iodine on his surgical area instead of mercurochrome and it had eaten away at the skin under the cast.

In today's medicine, the doctors would have been charged with a malpractice suit, but in those days, most people didn't know that such a thing was possible.

Chapter 9

Jenny recalled the evening she first set eyes on Russ. When she was seventeen, she was popular and attended many community club dances. That's where she was when she noticed 'him' across the room that October evening. She and her friend Adele giggled as Jenny ogled him. His tall, dark, handsome looks and football star build attracted her as soon as she spotted him. Jenny was tall herself and felt most comfortable when she dated tall men.

Russ was rather introverted and was not comfortable in such a noisy, bustling environment and knew he would probably leave early as usual when the chaos became too uncomfortable for him. He worked in an all-male environment, and had little chance to meet eligible women, so had gone outside his comfort zone by coming to the dance. When he first spotted Jenny across the room, his heart began beating like a trip hammer. Her tall good looks, slender but shapely legs and confident manner as she stood talking with several other girls made him want to meet her. When she sat down at her table, he decided to ask her to dance.

He and Jenny made eye contact across the room and Jenny watched as the gorgeous looking man kept eye contact with her as he walked over to her table. 'Hi, my name is Russ – would you like to dance?' he asked.

'I'd like that,' she replied as she smiled and rose from her chair – giving a sly look at Adele and rolling her eyes. They danced quite well together, and Jenny was glad she had worn high heels that night. Their dance turned out to be a spot dance. At the end of the dance when the head of the band walked across the dance floor seeking the spot he had chosen earlier Jenny and Russ were surprised when he stopped in front of them and gave them the prize.

What a beginning! she thought. They walked back to Jenny's table to see what they had won. It was a box of chocolates that they shared with others at their table.

Do you mind if I join you?' Russ asked.

Jenny nodded, 'Sure, have a seat.'

They sat together chatting and dancing for the rest of the evening. Although Jenny was still in high school, Russ was already working for the railway and she learned that he was two years older than she. He seemed so much more mature than the school kids she'd dated so far and appeared to have his life in order. After they danced the last dance, he asked 'Can I drive you home.'

Jenny nodded her head. This was another plus. Most of the boys she dated didn't have a car – but Russ did, and she was impressed especially when she saw his Ford Mustang sports car. When they got to her front door, Russ gave Jenny a quick peck on the cheek and asked, 'Would you go out with me tomorrow night? There's another dance at the Silver Heights Community Centre.'

Jenny nodded her head and said, 'Yes, that sounds great. What time does it start?'

'It starts at eight, so I'll pick you up about then. See you tomorrow.' he said as he waved goodnight and walked back to his car.

Russ picked her up the next night and they had a lovely evening at the dance. As they entered the community centre they were given an admission ticket and were told to keep it because there was going to be a door prize. Later that evening – to their surprise, they won the door prize. *This relationship is destined to be a success!* she thought.

Chapter 10

The July before she and Russ had met, Jenny was working as a typist in the typing pool at the Veteran's Hospital where Ian worked. Part of Jenny's job was to go into various wards of the hospital to collect the medical records that were typed by the women in the typing pool. Although it was a veteran's hospital, it also had younger military men as patients, and she often received wolf whistles as she walked down the halls of the wards.

She was given the responsibility of typing reports for the Recreation Department, and for several months had collected records from Bill Beckam. One morning her typing supervisor said, 'Jenny because you know basically how the Recreation Department works, I want to know if you would like to oversee looking after the Recreation Department while Bill is away on holidays for two weeks? He's asked if you can do it for him.'

Jenny was surprised that her supervisor thought she was mature enough at seventeen to take on such a monumental task. She knew how many responsibilities Bill had. But it was a wonderful opportunity for her, so she replied, 'Sure, I'll do it.'

The next day, Bill showed her how to record the recreational activities that were offered and who would take part in those activities. He had already ordered the bus for the upcoming football game, but she would have to check that it was the right size of bus to accommodate the final number of patients that had signed up.

He showed her another list he used to keep track of the needs of the patients. If a patient smoked, he was supplied with adequate cigarettes for his use while he was in the hospital. If he needed shaving lotion, a deck of cards, a comb or a housecoat, those too were supplied. 'You would have to keep track of all new patients while I'm gone.

You'll get their names every morning from the admissions department and visit their wards to interview them so you can get them anything they require. Here's a list of the things we can supply to them at no cost.'

On her first morning on the job, Jenny settled herself into Bill's office and got to work. She had her typewriter brought to the Recreational Department, so she could remain there in case someone needed to talk to her. The job required her to do a lot of paperwork and involved considerable interaction with the patients, but at the end of the two weeks, Jenny felt she had done an excellent job of staying on top of the paperwork and activities.

On the afternoon of the day Bill was supposed to return, a representative from the hospital Human Resources Department arrived at the door. Jenny had been puzzled that morning when she went to the Recreational Department and saw that Bill was not there.

The man said, 'I've just spoken with Bill, and he's advised us that he won't be back. He's been offered and has accepted a position in Vancouver and won't be back.'

Jenny didn't know what to say.

'We're wondering if you would look after the Recreational Department until we find a replacement?' he asked.

'I guess so. There haven't been any plans made for more sporting outings. I'll have to look over Bill's old records to see what kind of activities he normally schedules for this time of the year. But yes, I can do it.' she finally said.

That night she excitedly told Ian and Martha about her new assignment. Ian was particularly proud and went around the next morning to see Jenny in her new office.

On October 23rd the week she met Russ, the Hungarian revolt began in Budapest. A student demonstration mobbed the parliament buildings in Budapest and Soviet Security Police fired on the students. This initiated the Soviet retreat from Budapest. Many of those injured in that revolt were taken to other countries for treatment. A lovely Hungarian seventeen-year old student, Magda Zhukov was admitted with gunshot wounds to her leg and arm to a ward at Jenny's Veteran's Hospital. Her parents had been killed the day after she was shot so she had no one to care for her.

Jenny visited her to see if there was anything she needed. She knew that Magda did not speak English. Magda was approximately the same size as Jenny, was blonde and had the same pale skin colouring as she, so she'd prepared accordingly and came bearing gifts.

'Hello Magda. I'm Jenny.' she said pointing to herself.

'Jenny,' replied Magda.

First Jenny handed Magda a package of makeup she'd purchased for her.

Magda looked at it then glanced up at Jenny with tears in her eyes. It had been a terrorising time for her and she was overwhelmed by the kindness of the many Canadian people that had helped her. She held Jenny's hand and nodded her thanks.

Then Jenny handed her another package that was a lovely silk housecoat with matching slippers. The tears flowed again.

The next day, Jenny arranged to have a Hungarian interpreter come to help them communicate. The interpreter learned that Magda's fourteen-year-old brother Mikhail was still in Hungary and she was very fearful for his welfare. Through the interpreter, Jenny assured her that she would be contacting the Red Cross, so they could find out how he was.

Ten days later, Jenny entered Magda's room with a big surprise. Mikhail was all smiles as he greeted his sister. The Red Cross had flown him over and found a family willing to care for him and later for Magda after she recovered from her injuries.

It was after that incident that Ian spoke with Jenny, 'It looks as if the hospital is taking advantage of you. You've been working at a managerial level but are still paid as a typist. That's not right. I think you should apply for the position and if given it, should receive the same salary as Bill received.'

Jenny agreed and made an appointment to speak with the Human Resources Manager who had put her into the temporary position. Within two weeks, he hired another person to do the job. Jenny was so terribly disappointed that within a week, she'd applied for and was offered a new position as a secretary to a Wing Commander at the Air Force Base. Her boss was a lovely man who treated Jenny with respect and as if she was one of his daughters.

Chapter 11

Jenny and Russ were soon dating each other exclusively. Very early in their relationship Jenny made it plain to Russ that she had no desire to have sex before marriage. Like most virile males he made several attempts when he became too aroused during their occasional petting sessions, but never failed to stop going further when she said 'no.'

He bought her flowers, took her out to dinner and dancing and they had an active social life. They double-dated with his or her friends. Russ had two close friends who'd been his neighbours since they were toddlers. One was Grant Davidson. Grant had dated Betty since they were thirteen, and when she was sixteen she became pregnant and they married. Since then it seemed that Betty was either pregnant or nursing a baby and as Russ explained, they lived in an 'early poverty' style of home – nothing matched – everything was as cheaply bought as possible and they lived from paycheque to paycheque.

His second friend was Hugh McKenzie. Hugh was a close double to Elvis Pressley and had the same sensuous charm and good looks. When Jenny met him, she was overwhelmed by his good looks and could easily have fallen for him. However, she realised he was out of bounds because he and Doreen had recently announced their engagement. Another reason was that Doreen and Jenny had become good friends were respectful of each other and enjoyed each other's company. So, Jenny decided she would never chase Hugh even though she was attracted to him.

She and Russ double-dated with two of Jenny's friends, but Russ was not very friendly towards them and openly told Jenny he didn't want to go out with them again. Jenny was puzzled, because her friends were nice people, especially her best friend Adele Morrow. She had to content herself with seeing her girlfriends for lunch without Russ, but slowly but surely Jenny's friends drifted away.

Time passed quickly, and Jenny realised that a year had gone by since she'd met Russ. One Wednesday night in October when they were sitting watching television in her family's rumpus room, Jenny said, 'Do you realise that this is our anniversary? It's been a year since we met. The time has flown by so fast I can hardly believe it.'

Russ reached over and took her hand. 'I know it's a year, and I waited until tonight to ask you something.'

Jenny held her breath in anticipation – she thought she knew what he was going to say. When he asked, 'Will you marry me?' she was quick to say, 'Yes, I'll marry you!'

'When do you want to get married?' he asked as he gave her a big kiss and hug.

'Well because I'm just eighteen, people might think we 'had' to get married if we get married too soon. Why don't we plan on a June wedding? That way, we'll have time to prepare and won't have to rush things.'

Her parents were upstairs playing a card game called canasta. 'Shall we tell my parents?' she asked.

'Yes, why don't we.' he replied.

Jenny expected some resistance from her parents because she would still be eighteen in June, but she thought she was mature enough to get married. 'Mom, Dad we have something to tell you.' she said then noticed the look that passed between her parents. 'Russ has asked me to marry him and I've said yes. We wanted you to be the first to know.'

She watched her parents faces and could see their concern, so she continued, 'I know you think I'm too young and probably wonder if I'm pregnant – well I'm not. And we want to wait until June for the wedding. Please say you approve of us getting married.'

Ian and Martha looked at each other, nodded their heads and gave their approval.

'Oh, I'm so glad you approve,' she beamed as she hugged them both.

Her father stood looking up at Russ and shook his hand, 'Welcome to our family, son.'

Russ beamed, and his smile told it all.

'When are we going to tell your parents?' asked Jenny.

'Well, you're invited to my home tomorrow night for dinner – why don't we tell them then?'

Russ picked her up that Thursday night and before they went into his family home he gave her a big hug. 'I know you're worried about telling my parents – especially my Dad. But they both like you even though you aren't Italian. My dad always hoped that I would marry an Italian woman.'

Russ's father, Frank Carponi had been married before he met Russ's mother. Jenny learned later that this marriage had ended when his wife committed suicide. That marriage produced a son – Dario who at sixteen ran away from home shortly after his mother died. A few years later, Frank met and married Nellie Brown, a forty-year-old spinster who had just emigrated from England. Frank was five feet eight inches tall and Nellie was barely five feet tall, but two years later they produced a son, Russ, who grew and grew and grew until he was six feet four inches tall.

Nellie's brothers were all over six feet tall, so he obtained his genes from his mother's side of the family. Their second son, Antonio arrived eighteen months later. He had his father's genes and looked very much like his father and ended up the same height as his father.

It hadn't taken Jenny long to understand that Frank was supreme ruler of his family. His wife and two sons were expected to obey his every command. This didn't overly concern Jenny, because Russ acted very differently with her.

At dinner, the evening when they were going to announce their engagement, Jenny was apprehensive during the first part of the meal. She kept sneaking looks at Russ wondering when he was going to tell his family. His younger brother Antonio kept watching them, until he said,

'What's up with you two. You're acting very strange tonight?'

'Well, we do have an announcement to make.' said Russ, 'I've asked Jenny to marry me and she's said yes.'

For a while, nobody said anything until finally Antonio said, 'I had a feeling that's what was going on – welcome to the family Sis.' he stood up and came around the table to give her a big hug.

His parents were obviously not expecting this announcement and sat quietly at the table.

'Mom, Dad, what do you think about our decision?' prompted Russ. He could tell from their reaction that they were not happy about his announcement.

Frank looked at Russ and said, 'You're awfully young to think about getting married.' Then he turned with a scowl on his face and looked directly at Jenny, 'Are you pregnant?'

Nellie gasped and grabbed Frank's arm in reprimand. 'Frank, you don't ask a question like that!'

'It's okay Mom. 'No, she's not pregnant.' replied Russ. 'So people won't wonder about that, we aren't getting married until June. Now do we have your approval to get married?'

Jenny could tell that Russ was annoyed at his father's reaction and his facial expression announced it clearly. His father realised that Russ would go ahead with the marriage with or without his approval, so reluctantly decided to give his approval. It's not that he didn't like Jenny, but he'd expected Russ to marry an Italian woman. Instead, Jenny's lineage was from Scotland and Ireland.

Frank looked at Nellie – who nodded, and he replied, 'Yes, we give our permission. Now, let's get on with our meal.' he said dismissing any further conversation about the upcoming marriage.

Jenny felt slighted at his abrupt way of giving his approval. He had used the word 'permission' as if he was the one that decided whether they did or did not get married. He didn't seem to understand that they were both legally able to marry with or without parental approval. She knew that in his home he was 'lord and master' and his quiet unassuming wife obeyed him without question.

As Russ drove her home that night they discussed where they would live and what they would need to buy for their home. Russ explained, 'Most of my paycheque I give to my parents. The rest has been spent on buying and running my car and of course taking you out.'

'Do you have any money in a savings account?' Jenny asked.

'I have a couple of thousand dollars. Some of that will have to go towards your engagement ring and our wedding rings. How about you?'

'When I was younger I babysat a lot, and since I started my job last June, I've been able to buy my bedroom suite. It's a queen-sized bed with two dressers. I should have enough in my savings account to buy a kitchen and living room suite by the time we get married. And I think my parents will let me take the television set from my bedroom.'

Jenny and Russ sat down and made a budget of what money would be coming in and what they anticipated their expenses would be. They were sure they could manage somehow to buy whatever else they needed and of course there would be wedding presents from both sides of the family.

Later, Jenny's parents asked them whether they would like to rent the one-bedroom downstairs unit in a two-story rental property they owned in a nearby suburb. It was an investment property that they and their family had lived in a few years ago. When they moved out they divided the home into two suites, one upstairs and one downstairs. It sounded ideal and the monthly rental was within their means. Jenny knew that her parents could get much more rent than they were asked to pay and gave them a big hug when she confirmed that they would love to live there. Besides, she'd lived there before, so knew the neighbourhood and how to get around in that area of the city.

Soon, Jenny and her mother started making plans for the wedding.

'Do you want to buy your dress, or do you want me to make it?' Martha asked. Her mother was an accomplished seamstress and Jenny knew that she would do a good job of making it for her. After several weeks of examining bridal patterns they chose one that took advantage of Jenny's trim figure.

Her dress was made mainly of snowy white satin. Its strapless hand-embroidered bodice was beautifully fitted to the dipped waist. The skirt was full and the overskirt of white satin was gathered up in the front to the dipped waist and flowed downwards towards the sides and ended up in a short train. In the area below this overskirt was a full underskirt of meters of fine silk that had matching embroidery to the top. Being five feet seven inches tall, Jenny was able to wear high heels and still be much shorter than Russ. A shoulder-length veil attached to a smart cloche hat that showed off her beautiful features completed her outfit.

After completing Jenny's wedding dress, they both worked on sewing a going-away ensemble, several other new outfits for Jenny, and Martha's and Susan's wedding outfits.

Russ and his ushers wore white tuxedoes. His brother Antonio was best man and Jenny's brother Jeff and Hugh McKenzie were his ushers. Jenny's matron of honour was her best friend Adele Morrow and her bridesmaids were her cousin Ruby Connelly and Sylvia Collins. Her eight-year-old sister Susan was their flower girl and Ian gave the bride away.

The wedding went off without a hitch and everyone had a wonderful time. For the first time in many years all her father's brothers and sisters were together, along with some of their children and even grandchildren. His brothers Mark,

Jack, George and two sisters Jane McCaulley and Joan Henderson had come from distant cities. They did not know it but this was the last time all six of them would be together.

Jenny had met many of Russ's Italian relatives when she and Russ attended his cousin's wedding in Thunder Bay two months before their own wedding. She'd enjoyed meeting them and had fun dancing with all his cousins at the wedding. The male cousins seemed to vie for the opportunity of dancing with this blonde beauty that was soon to marry their cousin. Many of them were invited and came to Jenny and Russ's wedding and insisted on dancing with the bride.

Shortly after midnight Jenny threw her bridal bouquet (that Doreen caught) and Russ laughingly retrieved the garter from under her skirt and threw it for the men waiting to catch it. Hugh scrambled and was successful in catching it. Two weeks later Hugh and Doreen eloped and were already a married couple by the time Jenny and Russ returned from their honeymoon.

Then it was suddenly time to say goodbye to their family and friends. They all waved goodbye as they gathered around the limousine that drove off with the bride and groom. The couple would spend the night at The Fort Gary Hotel, next door to the train station. Because Russ worked for the railway and had a railway pass, they would leave the next day for their honeymoon train trip to Vancouver. Jenny's father had delivered their travelling bags to the train station, but they each had an overnight bag with them in the limousine.

Chapter 12

When they entered their honeymoon suite at The Fort Gary Hotel, Jenny was suddenly very shy. She and Russ had not had much to drink at their wedding. Jenny had been kept so busy dancing with relatives and friends that she had only wanted water or soft drinks because of her thirst. However, she was glad to see that the hotel had supplied a bottle of champagne for the honeymoon couple. Russ gestured towards the bottle and Jenny nodded her approval. He popped the cork and poured drinks for them. After they finished their first glass, Russ reached for her glass and placed it on the table. 'I've been waiting so long for this night. I want you so badly I ache.' he murmured as he snuggled into her neck.

'I have too.' she admitted, 'but I'm a bit scared too. I've never made love before.'

'That makes two of us!' he exclaimed. 'We make a good team, don't we?' he said as he laughed.

They both chuckled and shared another glass of champagne. 'Shall I get undressed?' she asked. He nodded and watched as she gathered her nightgown and toiletries and went into the bathroom. She brushed her hair and cleaned her teeth.

Jenny had shopped carefully for her satin nightgown and decided that it had to be symbolically white rather than a sexy black or red. When she slipped it over her head, she glanced at the mirror. The image staring back at her from looked frightened and her face had a pinched, nervous look to it. She forced herself to smile and taking a deep breath, she opened the door.

Russ's eyes lit up when he saw her in her beautiful nightgown and walked over to her. As he gazed at her, longing shot through him, in the same urgent way it always did whenever he was near her. He had never wanted a woman as much as he wanted her.

'You're so beautiful.' he said as he tilted her chin for a deep kiss. When he pressed his lips against hers, she opened her mouth slightly so that his warm tongue could enter. As he kissed her more deeply and passionately, she felt his hard manhood press almost painfully against her.

Unexpectedly, his kisses stopped. He quickly undressed, throwing his wedding outfit on the chair. Jenny stared apprehensively when she saw him standing naked before her. She had never seen a naked man with an erection before and Russ's manhood seemed very large to her. *How can that fit into my body?* she wondered sceptically.

He gazed at her beautiful slim but curvaceous body. Her breasts were young, taut under the satin of her gown and her nipples stood out clearly under the silky fabric. He stood back and slipped the nightgown straps over her shoulders. The gown slithered to the floor and lay like a shimmering pool of satin at her feet. The sudden cool air made her nipples stand fully erect and she shivered.

'You're getting cold,' he said as he lifted her and carried her to their marital bed.

He kissed her deeply. The blood rushed through him and his desire for her was overwhelming. He moved over her body and slipping his hands under her body, lifted her closer to him. He groaned as he spread her legs, clasping her buttocks tightly as he searched to find the entrance to her. He took her urgently, needing to be joined to her, needing to make them as one.

Jenny gritted her teeth and almost screamed with the sudden unexpected searing pain. Russ had not given her time to become ready for penetration. Her body had not produced the lubrication necessary to have painless intercourse. But Jenny didn't know this because she was a virgin and had no knowledge of how Russ should have prepared her for a pleasant introduction to intercourse. She felt him pumping in and out of her, each time causing her more and more pain until he moaned, became rigid and lay still. After he released her and lay back panting on the pillow, she lay beside him with tears streaming down her face and her body bruised, torn and bleeding. He seemed oblivious to the pain he had caused her and was still in the throes of sexual ecstasy.

Jenny reached for the box of tissue beside the bed, grasped several tissues and placed them on her throbbing body. She could feel something oozing from her body. As she rose from the bed, she saw the large red circle of blood on the sheets. She threw the covers back over the ugly stain then staggered into the bathroom, still quietly sobbing.

As she sat on the toilet letting the blood and semen flow into the toilet she sobbed and shivered with emotion. When she felt rid of it, she then wondered what she should do. Her clothing was still in the bathroom, so she reached for her panties and stuffed them with more tissue. A hotel chenille bathrobe hung on the back of the door so she put that on and wrapped it snugly around her. Then she flushed the toilet, lowered the toilet seat and painfully sat down. She sat there for about five minutes when she heard a quiet tap on the door. It was Russ.

'Can I come in?' he asked.

'Okay.' she replied quietly as she prepared to leave the room. Her mind was in a quandary, and she was shaking all over.

Russ stood aside as she stepped through the door. He closed the door and used the toilet. As he left the bathroom, he saw Jenny sitting on the end of the bed and heard her sobbing, 'What's the matter?' he asked as he examined her tearstained face.

She went to her side of the bed, pulled back the covers and pointed to the red circle in the bed. Russ gave her a puzzled look. 'Why did that happen?'

'You hurt me badly. Why did you have to be so rough? You know I've never made love before? Couldn't you wait a bit so I was ready for you?'

'I didn't know I would hurt you. I thought you enjoyed it as much as I did.'

'Well, I didn't and in the future, I hope you'll take more time to make sure I'm ready.' she sobbed. She went to the bathroom and returned with a bath towel that she placed over the red stain on her side of the bed. She was embarrassed to think what the hotel maid would think about the stain.

Climbing back into the bed, still in the housecoat, she turned her back on him. Russ placed his hand on her shoulder, but she shrugged it off. He gave up trying to placate her and was soon asleep and snoring loudly.

She hardly slept that night and was glad when morning came. After having a shower and getting dressed, she realised she was still bleeding. As she passed by Russ she said, 'I'm going downstairs to the little shop. I have to get something.'

She purchased sanitary pads to absorb the flow that was still coming from her body. The flow wasn't heavy, but she was terribly sore and had to force herself to walk normally.

When she returned to their room, Russ had already ordered breakfast from room service. She really didn't have much of an appetite but forced herself to eat. Because both sets of parents had promised to come to the train station to see them off that morning, she tried to make herself more cheerful, so they wouldn't know how upset she was. Her biggest concern was that Russ didn't seem to think he'd done anything wrong – that it was just because she was a virgin that she hurt so badly. She wondered if he could be right.

They checked out of the hotel and Russ carried their overnight bags next door to the train station. They'd just picked up their travelling luggage and put them on a trolley when Ian and Martha arrived. Russ and Jenny had just been contemplating whether they should find their compartment on the train, so were relieved to see them.

Martha noticed how pinched and white Jenny's face was and when she hugged her she asked quietly, 'Is everything all right?'

Jenny nodded, but the mother in Martha knew that something was terribly wrong. Unfortunately, she was not able to talk privately with her daughter before she left because it was soon time for Jenny and Russ to board the train and find their compartment. She gave Jenny another extra long hug trying to convey that she hoped she would be all right.

'We'll pick you up when you get back from your honeymoon,' Ian said as they boarded the train.

Just before boarding the train she and Russ searched the platform for his parents, but they did not arrive before their train left the station. Jenny could tell that Russ was very disappointed that they had not bothered to come as promised.

They liked their private compartment and found it cosy for their two-day trip. It had two benches that the steward folded down into a bed at night and it even had its own small bathroom. They both found it quite boring as the train travelled over the vast tundra of the prairies. They soon left Manitoba and entered Saskatchewan. You could see for miles and there wasn't much to see the land was so flat. Jenny was bored with the scenery so read a book she'd brought with her.

That night as they prepared for bed, Russ became amorous and obviously expected to have sex again. Jenny backed away shaking her head and said emphatically, 'None of that tonight – I'm still bleeding and I'm far too sore to do it again.'

After a perfunctory kiss, they lay back to back throughout the night. The next morning, they arrived in Calgary, Alberta and were able to spend an hour there while the train was refurbished. They strolled outside the station and were able to catch their first glimpse of the majestic Rocky Mountains. A dome car was added to the train and because they were in a compartment, they were able to sit in it as it travelled through the spectacular mountains. Jenny was enthralled at the lovely sight as they looked down on the Fraser Valley that seemed to be miles below them. From the window of their compartment, they were able to spot a black bear with her cubs, a massive elk with huge antlers and a small deer.

The next day they arrived in Vancouver station and were greeted by Ian and Martha's good friends Bob and Angel Switzer. They had a lovely home in North Vancouver and had offered them the use of the granny flat at the back of their property for their ten days in Vancouver. It was self-contained, and they could come and go as they pleased.

It took several days for Jenny to mend and stop bleeding and another day before her internal bruising went down. Russ kept asking whether she was well enough to try again and promised to be gentler with her. On the fourth day of their stay, Russ went to a pharmacy and bought some lubricating cream to see if that would help them. That night they tried again. Jenny was so apprehensive that she found herself tightening up so found that again she didn't enjoy it at all. The lubrication did help somewhat, but Russ still entered her far too soon, just minutes after they'd gone to bed. No foreplay except a few kisses – no romantic words, no caresses, no fondling, no stroking. Jenny kept thinking, *If this is love-making I don't like it at all!*

Although Jenny disliked the sex, she found she really enjoyed touring the sites around Vancouver. Bob and Angel were history buffs and loved showing Jenny and Russ the special sights in and around Vancouver. They had lunch at the prestigious Hotel Empress. As Bob drove them over the Burrard Bridge he explained that when it was built, it was one of the first high-level crossing bridges in Western Canada.

They also drove over the Lions Gate Bridge, Vancouver's most famous bridge that connected Vancouver to the North Shore. Like San Francisco's Golden Gate Bridge, the Lions Gate Bridge was a suspension bridge, and both bridges were partially built in Burnaby, British Columbia.

They visited Stanley Park, with its majestic cedar, hemlock and fir trees that teemed with wildlife. It encompassed over four hundred hectares close to the downtown core of Vancouver. They walked along the seawall, a popular walking and biking trail.

They visited Stanley Park, with its majestic cedar, hemlock and fir trees that teemed with wildlife. It encompassed over four hundred hectares close to the downtown core of Vancouver and walked along the seawall, a popular walking and biking trail.

Jenny and Russ also went on the Grouse Mountain Ski Lift high above the Douglas firs with again breathtaking views of the City of Vancouver, the Pacific Ocean, the Gulf Islands and the surrounding mountains.

Another afternoon they visited the Vancouver Aquarium, officially Canada's first public Aquarium that had opened just two years earlier in June 1956.

The day before they were to leave, they visited another suspension bridge. Only minutes away from downtown Vancouver, Capilano Suspension Bridge was another of Vancouver's famous landmarks. When Jenny saw the flimsy-looking bridge, she was reluctant to walk on it even though it offered a squirrel's eye view of the thriving coastal forest. It had a wooden plank base and cables at arm's height that people could hold onto as they walked over it. She put one foot on the bridge and stepped back quickly as it began to sway. When she looked down, it seemed that the water was hundreds of feet below the tiny little bridge. Angel assured her that it was safe and convinced her by walking on it for the first twenty feet, then stopped and beckoned to Jenny. Jenny took a big breath and ventured over the swinging, swaying bridge to the other side. She realised that she would have to back-track over the same hazardous-appearing bridge to return to the car park.

All too soon, their honeymoon holiday was over and it was time to head back to Winnipeg. The night before they left to get on the train, they took Bob and Angel out to dinner to show their appreciation for their hospitality. At the train station, they all promised to write and keep in touch.

Chapter 13

It was Saturday when they returned to Winnipeg. Ian and Martha greeted them at the train station and Ian helped Russ with the luggage. Martha had worried about Jenny the entire time she'd been gone and was glad to see that she looked better – not entirely happy – but better than she'd seemed at the beginning of their honeymoon.

'How was Vancouver?' she asked as she walked beside Jenny.

'Vancouver was wonderful Mom and your friends Bob and Angel Switzer were really great. They squired us around a lot. We went to all kinds of places – yes we had a great time.'

'And how are you?' her mother asked concern showing on her face.

Jenny shrugged her shoulders and said, 'I'll talk to you about it later, Mom.'

Her parents delivered them to their new home, the downstairs portion of a two-story rental property they owned. They introduced them to the couple, Patrick and Rayna Dorsett who rented the upper floor of the large home. While they were on their honeymoon, Ian had moved her bedroom suite into the home and Martha had been there when their new kitchen and dining room suites were delivered. They had left their wedding gifts on the new dining room table and elsewhere in that room Martha had also gone to the store and stocked the fridge with necessities – even two T-bone steaks they could have that evening for dinner. They didn't stay long but invited Jenny and Russ for dinner at their home the next evening.

The next day, when they arrived at her parent's home, Jenny and her mother went into the kitchen to prepare dinner. As Russ and her father walked through the kitchen her father asked Russ to help him with a problem he was having with his car. 'Call us when dinner's ready.' Ian said.

He knew that Martha was very concerned about Jenny and wanted the opportunity of speaking with her privately.

As soon as the men left for their garage, her mother took that opportunity to speak with Jenny. It was obvious that something had gone wrong and her mother was anxious to know if there was anything she could do to help.

'All right; we're alone. Now I want you to tell me what's going on. You looked like death the morning you left for Vancouver and I can't say you looked much better when you got back.'

Jenny hesitated, wondering how much she should tell her mother. Then she decided she had to speak to someone and probably her mother was the best one to talk to.

'Mom, you may or may not have known that I was a virgin when I got married.' she said shyly.

Her mother nodded her head. 'I was quite sure you were – but these days you never know.'

'Well I was and every sexual experience I've had since my wedding night has been horrible.' she said as tears started pouring down her face.

'What happened to make you feel this way?' she enquired.

Jenny told her the complete story and as she explained what had happened, Martha became more and more anxious. 'Is that the way sex is with you and dad?' Jenny asked.

'Oh goodness no! Your father is the best lover a person could ever have – so gentle, never expecting me to have sex unless we both want it. He always waits until I'm ready.' She said, her face a rosy red with embarrassment as she remembered that this was her daughter she was talking to.

'Then what happened with Russ that I hate it so much?' she asked tremulously.

'Honey, a man has to wait till a woman is ready to have intercourse otherwise all he's doing is relieving his own sexual tensions at the expense of his partner. You're going to have to insist that Russ take the time to make sure you're ready for sex. What he's doing to you is not lovemaking. It's pure sex!'

'Okay Mom. I'll talk to him about it. Maybe I can buy some books that explain how important it is for me to be ready. Thanks, Mom. I was embarrassed to speak to anyone about it, but I'm glad we had time to talk about this.' she said as she hugged her mother.

Meanwhile, Ian asked Russ, 'How was your honeymoon?'

'Oh, it was great. Your friends really showed us a good time, but still gave us the privacy we needed.' Russ replied.

'Jenny didn't look too good the day you left. I hope she didn't drink too much bubbly and was hung over.' Ian asked as he pointed to a tool he required.

'Oh no. She hardly drank anything at the wedding and we only had two glasses of champagne at the hotel.' he replied as he passed a spanner to Ian.

'Was she ill during the trip?' Ian asked.

'No, she was fine.' Russ wondered where Ian's questions were heading, then frowned as he considered, 'Could Jenny had told her parents about their sexual problems?'

Ian saw that Russ was becoming upset, so decided not to delve more into the situation. Russ was glad when Ian changed the subject and began discussing the problems he was having with his car.

When they joined their spouses for dinner, Ian was glad to see that Jenny looked better. He knew that she and Martha must have taken the opportunity to discuss whatever problem had been bothering Russ and Jenny. He also knew that Martha would share the problem with him. Later when Jenny and Russ had left, she did discuss it with him and he was furious about the rough way Russ had abused Jenny.

A week later, Jenny made an appointment with Russ's doctor to be fitted for a diaphragm, so she wouldn't become pregnant. As he examined her he noticed the tear in her vagina and asked her about it. She shyly explained what had happened on her wedding night and asked him if there were any books about intercourse and foreplay.

He shook his head in sympathy, 'This should never have happened. I'm sorry you had such a sad introduction to intercourse. Here are two books I think you should buy or borrow from the library. You need to emphasise to Russ that his total disregard for you during intercourse in interfering with your love life.'

Jenny bought and read the recommended books. Suddenly she understood how intercourse should really be between a couple and realised how selfish Russ was being by not waiting until she was ready.

The next Wednesday night when they went to bed and Russ reached for her, she held him off. 'We have to discuss things. I saw your doctor earlier this week to be fitted for a diaphragm. He asked me about the tear I had in my vagina and said that it would not have happened if you had taken the time to prepare me for intercourse. He's recommended that we read these books.'

She showed him a chapter she'd read that would help him understand what he needed to do to help her become aroused. He read it and promised to change. When Jenny mentioned that she was turned on by some men's cologne, Russ replied, 'You don't expect me to wear that sissy stuff do you?'

Russ did try and improved somewhat but he still hurt her because he was so rough when he tried to stimulate her with his hands. He never took enough time, nor did he do anything romantic to put her in the mood. He never complimented her about how she looked or for all the things she did to make his life comfortable. His efforts didn't seem to do much to improve the situation for Jenny and he soon reverted to his 'wham bam, thank you ma'am' habit of having sex.

During her marriage, Jenney never reached a climax during intercourse with Russ. However, during her visit with the doctor, he had encouraged her to masturbate to bring herself to a climax and she had to accept that this was the only way she could alleviate the sexual tensions that often built up in her body.

Chapter 14

The Monday after Jenny and Russ returned from their honeymoon they both had to return to work. Jenny worked from eight to four o'clock and Russ worked the four to twelve shift so they didn't see each other at night except Wednesday and Thursday evenings, and Saturday and Sunday during the day.

That morning, Jenny prepared their breakfast and was just heading out of the kitchen to leave for work when Russ tapped his spoon on the side of his coffee mug. At their wedding, people had tapped their spoons on the side of their wine glasses, which meant that the bride and groom had to kiss. 'Okay, one kiss - then I have to go.' Jenny said.

'No, I don't want a kiss – that was to tell you I want another cup of coffee.'

Jenny aimed an astounded look at him. She couldn't believe what he'd said.

'Russ, we're in a partnership now. We both work, so we both pitch in at home. If you want another cup of coffee – there's the coffee pot – help yourself.' she added disgustedly as she snatched up her purse and left for work.

She soon learned that Russ was hopeless around the home. His mother had made his bed, picked up after him and had done everything around the home to make him comfortable. It was soon clear that he expected the same behaviour from Jenny. He'd come home from work and step out of his work clothes and leave them lying on the floor. If they went out socially, he left those clothes over the back of a chair.

The Thursday evening after they returned from their honeymoon, Hugh and Doreen Mackenzie came over for a post-wedding dinner. By now he and Doreen were married and they had a lovely wedding gift for them.

Before they arrived, Jenny was kept busy preparing the meal, setting the table and getting dressed. She'd waited an entire week for Russ to pick up his clothes but saw that they were still lying all over their bedroom. Disgustedly, she went to the back porch, got a large black garbage bag and stuffed Russ's clothes into it including his suit. Then she disgustedly threw the bag into their clothes closet. Two days later, Russ asked where all his work clothes had gone – that he didn't have any clean ones left.

'Where did you leave them?' asked Jenny innocently.

'In our bedroom.' he replied

'Where in the bedroom?' she said as she stood with her hands on her hips.

'In that corner.' he said as he pointed to the corner he normally threw his work clothes.

'Don't you know where dirty clothes belong? The laundry basket is in the basement next to the washing machine. And did you expect me to hang up your suit?'

'Well, where are my clothes?' he asked as he peered around the room.

'I only had a few minutes to clean up your mess when Hugh and Doreen came over on Thursday. I couldn't leave our bedroom with your clothes all over the room when they came, so I put all the things you'd left lying around in a plastic bag. It's in the closet.' she said as she pointed to the closet then added, 'Clothes do not magically get clean; magic hands don't take them away to wash them and return them all ironed and hanging up. The least you can do is put them in the laundry basket, I'll do the rest.'

After that, he improved a bit, but always acted as if it was an imposition – not his job to clean up after himself. There were all sorts of household duties to sort out between them. With lots of resistance and complaint, they found a system for clearing up, doing laundry and shopping.

When they purchased a dishwasher, Jenny automatically took her dishes and placed them in the dishwasher. Russ left his where they were on the table and they were still there when he came to breakfast the next morning. 'Why did you leave these dishes on the table?' he asked.

'I didn't – you did. I put mine in the dishwasher. I guess you forgot to put yours in there before I washed the rest of them.'

Shortly after her marriage, Jenny realised that their life had changed in many other ways. Their social life was not what it had been before their marriage. She kept encouraging Russ to do the things they had done before they were married, but he kept explaining that they didn't have to do those things any more – that they were married. Why buy her flowers when they had some in their garden? Why take her out for dinner, when they could have it at home? Why should they go dancing when he hated dancing?

Four months after their marriage Russ reluctantly promised Jenny that they would go out to dinner the following Saturday night. He arranged to change shifts with a co-worker, so they could have Saturday and Sunday nights off for a change.

About three o'clock that Saturday afternoon, Jenny started preparing for their night out. After having a leisurely bath using scented bath salts, she fixed her hair in a special way, and slipped into her sexiest dress. By five o'clock, she was ready. Their restaurant reservation was for six so they would have to leave soon.

She went down into Russ's basement workroom and asked, 'When are you going to have a shower and change?'

'What for?' he asked suddenly noticing she was all dressed up.

'We've got a dinner reservation in one hour.'

'Well, we can't go. I'm in the middle of something and don't want to leave it.'

'Are you telling me we aren't going out for dinner after you promised me we would?'

'That's right.' he said as he turned away from her and continued sanding the piece of wood he was working on.

'When you give me your word, I expect you to keep it!' she threw at him as she climbed the basement stairs.

She now knew that she had not paid enough attention to the warnings she should have recognised when she met Russ – how different his upbringing was from the family life she'd enjoyed before her marriage. He expected to be 'Lord and master' of his home and Jenny was having none of it.

Jenny checked her purse to make sure she had some money, phoned the restaurant, cancelled their reservation and walked to the nearby bus stop. *Where can I go?* she wondered, then decided she would visit Adele and her husband Jim. She wished she'd had an opportunity to phone to warn her that she was coming but decided to take the chance that it would be all right. If they weren't home, she would just go to a movie.

It took three busses, but she finally arrived at Adele's home. Adele answered the door and immediately could see that Jenny was upset. 'Come in.' she said as she opened the door.

'What's the trouble?' she asked as she noticed that Jenny was all dolled up.

Jenny explained what had happened and Adele said. 'Jim and I will be having a couple over for dinner. They'll arrive soon. You're very welcome to join us.'

'Oh no. I couldn't do that.' Jenny replied as she stood up to leave.

Adele pushed her back onto the sofa. 'Oh yes you are. You're staying for dinner. No arguments.'

Their friends Jessie and Aaron Millar arrived and the five of them had a lovely evening. Several times Jenny attempted to go home but was encouraged to stay longer. When it was time to go, Aaron offered to drive her home. 'It's not much out of our way – and it will save you the long trip home.'

So, they drove her home. Jenny peeked at her watch along the way and realised that it was after midnight. As they drew up to her front door, she saw a light on in their front window and with a sigh entered the front door. She was not looking forward to what she knew would either be glaring silence or an argument.

There was nobody home, even though the lights were on and she thought she'd seen a shadow through the front window. She prepared for bed and had just turned out the light when Russ came in. He was furious, and she could tell from his breath that he had been drinking.

'Where the hell have you been?' he bellowed.

'Out.' she replied, just as angrily.

'Who were you out with? I saw you arrive in some guy's car. Don't deny it.'

'You were home then when I arrived?' she countered.

'Never mind that – who is he?' he shouted.

'It was they – Jessie and Aaron Miller.' she said as she turned over in bed away from him.

'Well you're not going to get away with it.' he said as he roughly turned her over. He was astride her before she could move. He ripped away her silk pyjama bottoms, but she was so mad that she was determined that he would not rape her again.

'Do you get enjoyment out of raping your wife?' she screamed. 'Does it make you feel manlier, if you take me by force?'

He gave her a shove and crawled off her. That night he slept on the sofa in their living room.

Chapter 15

The next morning the air was frigid. They were to have dinner at his parent's place that night and because he had promised his father he would help him dig his garden, they'd left their home shortly after having their lunch. As soon as they arrived at his parents' place, Russ went into the back yard to help his father. Jenny was left with his mother, Nellie. Nellie was rather a chatterbox and with Jenny's raging headache she didn't want to be rude to her mother-in-law. She loved the woman but couldn't tolerate her constant chatter – not today anyway.

'I promised a friend that I would stop in and see her this afternoon. Seeing Russ is busy this afternoon, it will be a good time for me to go see her.'

Jenny got in their car and drove to Adele's home that wasn't far from her in-laws' place. She wasn't home, so Jenny went to a fast food place and had a cup of tea. She returned to her in-laws home less than an hour after she'd left. As she drove into the yard, she saw that everyone was gathered around the back door of the home. Russ's dad, Frank strode over as Jenny was exiting the car.

'What are you doing driving Russ's car without his permission?' he shouted.

Just what I need. she thought. She'd just calmed herself down but was instantly angry again. How dare this old man tell her what to do!

'This is now my car as well as Russ's, and I have every right to drive it whenever I want to.' she tried to say calmly.

'Russ bought it, so he owns It.' was Frank's curt retort.

'So, I suppose he should ask my permission every time he sleeps in the bed I bought or eats at the kitchen table or sits on the sofa I bought?' she roared back.

Russ suddenly stepped between them. He was still furious at Jenny for what she'd done the night before,

'Don't you dare talk to my father that way!' he shouted at Jenny as he lifted her bodily from the ground.

His fingers gripped her upper arms so tightly she couldn't move. He carried her this way for fifty feet until he reached the public sidewalk at the front of his parent's home. He placed Jenny's feet roughly on the ground, turned her around, and kicked her in the buttocks with his work boots. 'Get out and stay out!' he bellowed.

No one in his family had attempted to intervene between them. Jenny thought that at least Antonio would have stepped in to help her. She staggered a few steps then regained her balance and kept walking away from Russ – tears streaming down her face. Her purse was still in the car, so she had no money. What was she going to do? Where was she going to go? She just knew she couldn't go back to his parent's home. When she got to the corner of the street, she peered back to see whether anyone had followed her. No one had.

Her own parents lived about ten blocks away, so she started walking towards their home. She noticed that Russ's fingernails had pierced the backs of both her upper arms and they now had rivulets of blood running down them. As she passed a filling station, she decided to ask whether she could use their washroom facilities to clean up her arms and use their phone to call her parents.

The elderly male attendant at the filling station took one look at the distraught young woman and immediately thought *Rape. This girl has been raped.* and rushed over to assist her. She was as pale as a ghost and he led her to a chair behind the counter and brought her a glass of water. Everyone in the place was staring at her. The man asked a female customer to get some wet paper towels from the washroom, so he could clean up her arms. Then he went to the first aid kit in the staff room, applied a disinfectant and carefully dressed her wounds.

'Thank you so much,' murmured Jenny. 'Would you please let me use your phone? I want to phone my parents.'

'Of course you can. Do you want me to call the police?' he asked.

Jenny gave the man a startled look then suddenly understood why he'd said what he did. 'No, that's not necessary. My parents will look after this.'

Jenny didn't want anyone at the filling station to know what had happened to her, so when Martha answered the phone she said, 'Mom I'm at Jackson's filling station on Davidson Road. Can you please pick me up right away?'

Martha could hear from Jenny's voice that something was dreadfully wrong but didn't question her. 'I'll be right there.'

Martha arrived in record time and was upset to see Jenny in such a condition. 'What happened?' she asked the attendant.

'We don't really know. She just walked in here asking to use the washroom and phone. But she had blood running down both arms and looked as if she was going to pass out. I've cleaned the wounds and dressed them. I hope she'll be all right.' replied the concerned attendant.

'Well thank you for taking such good care of her,' added Martha.

As soon as they were driving, Jenny told her mother everything that had happened since the evening before and as soon as they arrived home Martha phoned Ian at work. He worked only minutes away and came right home. Jenny explained again what had happened. 'Do you want me to drive you home to get some of your clothes?' he asked.

'I don't have my purse, so don't have the keys to get in.' she replied.

'That's all right. Seeing we're your landlord, we have an extra set.'

They quickly drove over to Jenny's home, retrieved a suitcase from the garage that Jenny filled with work, casual clothes and toiletries. She saw her father glancing at the torn pyjama bottoms that were still lying in their bedroom floor and shook his head. 'I'll kill him if he ever hits or harms you again!' he raged.

'Dad, since you gave us the portable TV, I think we'd better take that with us.'

'Okay. Now let's get out of here. I don't want to run into Russ the way I feel right now. It could get very nasty.' he added indignantly.

They left, and Jenny returned to her parent's home. They put her things into her old bedroom and she slept well that night. Martha phoned the filling station and thanked them again for looking after her daughter. She didn't elaborate on what had happened – just thanked the attendant for his kindness.

The next morning, Jenny returned to work, but made sure she wore a long-sleeved outfit so her bandages would not be visible. The Air Force base was not far from her parent's home, so in good weather she was able to walk to work. As Wing Commander Warren passed her desk on Monday morning, he noticed that she seemed to be upset about something. He beckoned to her to come into his office, and then closed the door. 'You look so sad today. Is there anything I can do to help? Do you need some time off?'

'Oh no, just some trouble at home – it will settle down soon, but thanks for your concern.' she replied. He was such a kind man.

He nodded and repeated, 'Just remember if I can help in any way, just let me know.' She nodded as she rose from the chair and returned to her desk.

For six days she didn't hear from Russ. Finally, that Saturday morning he phoned. Ian answered the phone when he called.

'Can I speak to Jenny please?' Russ wanted to know.

'I doubt if she wants to talk to you after what you did to her.' was Ian's reply.

'I want to apologize to her for my behaviour and ask her to come home.' he said earnestly.

Ian turned away from the phone, 'Jenny, do you want to talk to Russ?'

First, she shook her head, but when her father told her what Russ had said, she agreed to speak with him.

Russ repeated his apologies and told her that such a thing would never happen again. 'Can I come over to see you?'

Jenny looked at Ian, 'He wants to come over to see me.'

'Just remind him that your mother and I will be here, and he'd better not start any trouble.' he added worriedly.

Russ promised he wouldn't and arrived a short time later. Even though Ian was six inches shorter and many pounds lighter than he, Russ was intimidated by the man and almost turned back instead of ringing the bell. However, he built up his courage and rang the bell. Ian met him at the door and ushered him into the living room. Jenny and her mother stayed in the kitchen. Ian stood before Russ and said plainly and clearly, 'If you ever harm my daughter again, so help me I'll make you wish you weren't alive!'

Russ nodded his head, 'I promise I will never harm her again. Now can I talk privately with her?'

'Yes, but remember we'll be in the next room.' was Ian's reply as he glared at Russ.

'Okay.' Russ said as he looked at the carpet.

Ian went to fetch Jenny and she squared her shoulders before she left the kitchen. She was apprehensive about being in the same room with Russ, knowing the kind of a temper he'd revealed to her that past Sunday afternoon. But when she entered the room she saw that Russ was sitting on the sofa with his head in his hands sobbing. He looked up when she entered the room with such anguish on his face, that she couldn't remain furious with him.

He stood up and cautiously approached her, 'I'm so sorry I hurt you. I shouldn't have done what I did either Saturday night or Sunday. Did I hurt you very much?' he asked as he started examining her.

She'd waited till that morning to take the bandages off her arms, but the marks and bruises still looked very sore and tender. 'Oh my God.' he said as he looked at them. 'I can't believe I did that to you!'

'Well you did, and I need you to promise that you'll never do anything like that again.' she admonished him.

'I do. I do. Can you ever forgive me?' he said contritely.

'I'll forgive you this time, but I will walk out for good if you ever hurt me again.' was Jenny's emphatic reply.

Jenny gathered her things, gave her parents a big hug and went home with Russ. Before she left, she told her parents that Russ was truly sorry and had promised that he would never harm her again. Ian just shook his head as he said, 'Time will tell. Time will tell.'

For a while they went out socially the same as they had before their marriage. Russ bought her flowers, told her he loved her and spent much more time with her. The only thing that didn't improve was their sex life.

At first Jenny refused to go to Russ's parent's home for their usual Sunday noon meals, but after several weeks Russ begged her to go, so she relented. Jenny and Frank were never destined to be close. Frank had refused to apologise for his outburst and Jenny certainly wasn't going to give in to the tyrant. She had to steel herself before each visit, telling herself that she wouldn't argue with him. Frank and Jenny seldom if ever spoke directly to each other and you could cut the air with the hostility between them. Nellie sat looking from one to the other shaking her head and was upset that their feud was not resolved.

Within two months, everything in their life went back to the way it had been before their separation and Jenny realised their honeymoon was over and the man she married, was not the man she thought she'd married. Because they seldom went out socially and their friends had drifted away, Jenny was very lonely and seriously thought about leaving Russ.

However, she did enjoy her job as secretary to Wing Commander Warren. He was kind and thoughtful to her and the other staff. Once he apologised to Jenny when he realised that she would have to file a document that had comments on it that annoyed him. He had written the word 'balls' over the document and Jenny was touched that he was so sensitive.

On occasion Jenny took dictation from two squadron leaders in the section. Squadron Leader Henderson was a staid middle-aged gentleman who always appeared to be standing at attention. He was very proper in his behaviour with his staff, but always insisted that every 'T' was crossed and every 'I' was dotted. Jenny learned to double-check everything she did for him.

Then there was Squadron Leader Patton. For some reason Jenny did not like this man. He seemed to have a smarmy, paternalistic attitude towards women in the department. One day he stopped by Jenny's desk and asked her to come to his office to take a letter for him. Jenny nodded, picked up her shorthand notebook and followed him down the hallway to his office. When he entered his office behind her, he closed the door and Jenny was astonished to see that he also locked the door. She sat apprehensively as she waited for him to start dictating the letter to her. Instead he stood behind her and placed his hands on her shoulders. Jenny stiffened in protest and when he slid his hands down to her breasts. She could hear his breath in her ear as he placed his face beside hers. Her heart began thudding so hard she could feel it in her head.

"What should I do?" she wondered.

Then her shock turned to rage. She took a breath and in a steely voice said, 'Take your hands off me or I will scream blue murder.'

He released his hands and Jenny bolted to the door, unlocked it and almost ran down the hallway to her desk. Her heart was pounding so hard her vision blurred and she was afraid she was going to pass out. Her first intention was to go to her desk until she recovered from the shock, but instead found herself swerving left until she stood at the doorway of Wing Commander Warren's office. He was in a meeting with two other officers, but when he looked up and saw Jenny's white, shocked face and heard her quavering voice as she said, 'I need to speak with you sir.' he stood up and said to the other men, 'We'll have to continue this later today. I'll phone you when we can get together.'

Jenny stood to the side of the door, even more upset because she had barged into her boss's office when he was in the middle of a meeting. The men passing by her gave her curious glances. They could see that there was something drastically wrong and hoped the Wing Commander would enlighten them later when they met again.

Wing Commander Warren came over and stood beside Jenny, and gently took her arm to guide her into his office. She peered up at him, wide-eyed and teary and said, 'I'm sorry sir. I didn't realise that you were in a meeting.'

'It's okay Jenny. What's wrong? Come and sit down.' he said as he led her to a chair that had just been vacated by his visitors. He looked again at Jenny, then went to the door of his office and closed it. It was obvious that Jenny was terribly upset by something and he was determined to give her privacy while she explained it.

'Sir, I can't … do work any more for Squadron Leader Patton. If I must, I will have to give you my notice.' she hiccupped the words out.

'What happened?' he asked full of concern.

Jenny explained what had happened and watched as his face changed from the kindness he had shown her into a rigid mask. She wondered if he was mad at her, but his next comment reassured her. 'You will never have to do work for him in the future and neither will any of the other secretaries. I want you to stay right here until you feel better. I'm going to talk to him right away.'

Jenny sat in the chair taking big breaths wondering what he was going to say to the man who had molested her. It wasn't long until she heard his angry voice from down the hallway as he chastised the man. Even though the door was closed in Squadron Leader Patton's office, his voice carried along the hallway to where Jenny was sitting. His anger prevented him from keeping his voice down. 'How dare you act that way with any female employee? From now on you will type and file your own letters and I will be reporting this to the proper authorities.'

Jenny realised that most of the people in the department must have heard the shouting. When the Wing Commander returned to his office, Jenny looked shyly at him. She had never seen him angry before. He sat at his desk and took several deep breaths then said, 'I guess we've both had a rotten time of this. I don't remember losing my temper like that for several years. I hope I didn't frighten you.'

'No sir,' she replied. 'I was just pleased that you believed me when I told you what had happened.'

'Well, it's over now. Please let me know if he tries anything again like that in the future.' he said as he rose and kindly patted Jenny on the shoulder.

'I'll get back to work now.' said Jenny. 'I was in the middle of typing the report you gave me this morning. I'll finish it now that I've calmed down. Thank you for being so understanding.' she added as she stood up and left the room.

The office was buzzing with gossip about what had happened, and Jenny just wished it hadn't happened. Several asked her what had happened, but she refused to talk about it. Soon their interest went to other things and the office returned to normal. Squadron Leader Patton was disciplined, transferred to another post and chastised not to use such behaviour in the future.

And then Jenny had her car accident.

Chapter 16

Jenny had not had sex with Russ (she refused to think of it as lovemaking because it wasn't) since before he'd been admitted to hospital with pneumonia and Jenny'd had her accident. She wondered, *Will I ever have enough feeling in my lower body for us to have sex again even though I don't enjoy it? Will Russ stay with me if we can't?*

She needn't have worried, because six weeks after her accident Russ made it clear that he intended to continue having sexual relations with her whether she was capable of participating or not. He didn't consult her about this or even hug or kiss her before entering her. That night he simply climbed over her, parted her legs, lifted her hips and dove into her. Jenny just lay there in shock.

He knows I feel nothing, but he still does this. she thought as he rammed into her. *It seems that his own sexual release is far too important to him to allow me to participate in any way.*

'Would it hurt you too much to at least pretend I'm part of this sex act?' she asked after he was sated.

'What do you mean?' he asked

'You could at least hug me or kiss me to let me be part of your sexual release!' she added.

He could see in the dim light that she was furious and vowed to do better next time. However most of the time she was asleep when he got home from work, so he neglected following through with his promise. He just climbed aboard her, sometimes even before she was awake and relieved himself.

Many times, the first inkling Jenny had that he was even home was when he groped her and took off her pyjama bottoms. Most of those times, she was too sleepy or didn't have time to get up and insert her diaphragm. The inevitable happened. Eighteen months after their marriage, one year after her accident and six months after she'd started recovering movement in her feet, Jenny realised she could be pregnant.

Her family doctor, Dr. Sims examined her and confirmed she was pregnant.

'How will I manage?' she asked apprehensively.

'You're improving so much with your therapy, that you'll manage all right.' he reassured her.

Russ was so excited when she told him that night. You'd have thought he'd performed a miracle. Later Russ marvelled when he first felt their baby move through Jenny's abdomen. Nellie was also enthralled. She'd never felt either of her babies move nor had she felt them externally with her hand. Nellie had been overweight before, during and after her pregnancies so Jenny surmised that the layers of fat kept her from feeling such a miracle.

As Jenny progressed through her pregnancy, she realised that there really wasn't room in their one bedroom rented home for a baby. She secretly checked the paper for a bargain home and found a small two-bedroom home that would need some work but would be fine for their growing family. That evening she told Russ about the home she had found.

'We can't afford to buy a home,' was his simple reply.

'That's where you're wrong.' Jenny said excitedly. 'With the down payment I'm able to put on it, our mortgage payments would be the same as our rent payments are now and it will be a bigger home.'

'What down payment? You know we don't have much in our joint savings account.' he exclaimed.

'Well, I have an account of my own that I opened with the money I received from the settlement from my car accident. There's more than four thousand dollars in that account. We can use that for the down payment.' she said excitedly.

They went to see the home, purchased it and moved in a month later. It was only three blocks away from Russ's parents' home. Sadly, for Nellie, Russ, and Antonio, Frank was diagnosed with pancreatic cancer and died five months later, before his first grandchild was born.

Jenny had an uneventful pregnancy but as she progressed with her accident recovery, she felt more sensations in her lower extremities and back. She suffered with terrible back pain and was often in tears as she fought the pain. This did not stop her from continuing her physiotherapy and she kept gaining extra movement in her feet and legs.

She kept wondering when her baby was going to be born. His birth date was predicted to be in mid-August, but that time came and went. Jenny was so huge she felt like a beached whale and wondered if her baby could be twins rather than just one baby. Finally, on the first day of September, she went into labour. Her first labour pain was at seven-thirty in the evening, and she started timing her contractions. By nine o'clock she realised that they were only five minutes apart and narrowing fast. Russ drove her to the hospital. When Dr. Sims examined her, he explained that it was just one big baby she was carrying, and he expected her to be in labour for some time. Their son Mark was born just before midnight. He was nine pounds six ounces, so was a large baby to have been born after only four and a half hours of labour. Jenny thought how ironic it was that he arrived on what Canadians celebrate as 'Labour Day.'

Dr. Sims delivered the baby and after she was settled in her room he explained, 'Your delivery was likely quicker because you had a large tear at the entrance to your vagina that was never repaired.' he added, 'I've repaired that tear, so you might feel sore for a few days.'

Jenny was too embarrassed to tell her doctor that the tear had happened on her first sexual experience. The nurse arrived with a bundle in her arms. She jokingly said, 'We searched all over the ward for a newborn with your name tag on it – but all we could find was this two-month old beauty.'

It was true. Mark did not resemble most newborns. His flesh was filled out and when he looked at Jenny, she was sure he was focusing his eyes on her. He was a model baby – very happy and contented. She nursed him until he was eight months old then on a regular visit to his paediatrician, he advised her to stop nursing him. Mark was a strapping baby who was thriving well, but Jenny had become a bag of bones because she'd lost so much weight. Her frail frame was unable to take the extra burden of nursing and looking after Mark while still in a wheelchair.

Disappointed at having to do so, Jenny stopped nursing Mark and the next month started taking birth control pills. It wasn't long until she realised that she'd waited one month too long and found herself pregnant again. Russ was so proud – as if it somehow it proved *his* fertility.

This time, her morning sickness was so severe that Dr. Sims prescribed medication to try to ease her discomfort. One Sunday night, a month later, she was watching television when she learned that babies were being born with deformities and that a new anti-nausea medication called Thalidomide was being taken off the market. Doctors were advising women who had taken the drug to see their doctors and possibly have abortions. Jenny had used up all her medication and had thrown away the container, so didn't know whether that was the medication she'd been prescribed. She hated to bother Dr. Sims at home on a Sunday night, so spent a sleepless night wondering if her baby could be born deformed. She called his office first thing Monday morning and was put through to Dr. Sims right away.

'I was in the process of phoning all the women who had been prescribed anti-nausea medication to let them know that I have never prescribed Thalidomide to my patients. So your baby is safe.' he announced with a smile.

'Thank goodness. I really had a rough night wondering if the baby would be all right. I understand some women are having abortions because the drug is likely to cause severe deformities.' she queried.

'Yes, sadly that's true, but in your case, it wasn't prescribed.' he said emphatically.

'Thanks Dr. Sims. I feel very relieved.' she added gratefully.

Jenny hadn't phoned Martha about her fears the night before but phoned her right away. 'Oh my God.' she replied. 'You were certainly lucky, weren't you?'

When Jenny first recognised that the flutter she was feeling in her abdomen, was made by her baby, she was very excited and told Russ about it. During her pregnancy with Mark, she had not had enough feeling in her abdomen to feel such a light flutter. After her morning sickness was over, Jenny's pregnancy progressed normally.

Jenny and Russ examined their home and realised that there really wasn't room for two babies in their home as it was now, so Russ started renovating their home. The living room was large, but what would soon be Mark's and the new baby's bedroom was quite small, so he decided to move the living room wall and make that bedroom larger.

Jenny had to be very careful to make sure Mark didn't eat any sawdust off the floor or grab one of Russ's dangerous tools. It was a trying time, because their home was not very large, and there wasn't much room where she could pen Mark up and keep him safe.

Russ was still remodelling their living room but was at work when Jenny heard Mark's sudden terrified scream. She rushed into the bedroom that was being renovated and quickly analysed what had happened. Russ had failed to replace the cover on an electrical outlet and Mark had somehow put his tiny fingers around the socket making an electrical connection. He was getting jolt after jolt of power and his little body jerked every time one surged through his body. Jenny rushed over to Mark, pushed herself out of her wheel chair onto the floor so she wouldn't be near metal and pulled his hand out of the socket.

She and Mark ended up lying on the floor a few feet away from the outlet. Jenny realised that she too had received a terrible shock just by pulling Mark's hand out of the socket. They both lay on the rug sobbing; Mark because he had received several jolts of electricity and she because her son had been hurt and knowing that the shock could have harmed her unborn baby.

As soon as she had comforted Mark, she phoned Martha. 'Mom I need your help. Russ left the cover off an electrical outlet and Mark has received several jolts of electricity. I had to pull his hand out of the socket, so I got a shock too. Can you come and take us to the hospital emergency ward?'

Her mother replied, 'We'll be right there.'

In record time her parents arrived. Ian drove, and Martha held Mark as he continued to cry. In the emergency ward they were taken into two separate curtained rooms and two doctors dealt with their injuries. The paediatrician, Dr. Williams, examined Mark while Ian stayed in the room with him. Dr. Sims attended to Jenny and Martha stayed with her. Jenny kept glancing over towards the curtain around Mark and asking, 'Is he all right? Is he all right?'

Mark had cried the entire drive to the hospital, so she was afraid that he had been injured more than she'd originally thought. The only sign of injury she could find before they left for the hospital was a small burn on his left hand. By now, Jenny knew that Mark was left-handed, so hoped there were no serious injuries to his hand.

'He's going to be fine – just some minor burns on his hand.' said Dr. Williams. 'He's had a terrible fright. There's no damage to his nerves and he seems all right mentally as well. But as a precaution, we'll keep him under observation overnight in case there's something we've missed. But I think he'll be fine.'

Dr. Sims examined Jenny – listening carefully to the baby's heartbeat. 'The baby's heartbeat is a little fast, but that's understandable after the shock it's received. Your heartbeat is fast too, but that too is understandable after the shock you've received and the worry it's caused. We won't know whether there's been any serious damage to the baby until it's born, but it's likely the baby will be fine. We'll monitor your pregnancy every week from now on.'

'So, we won't know for six weeks or so whether the baby has been damaged by the shock I received?' she said with concern.

'Unfortunately, no we won't. But it's likely the baby will be fine. We'd also like to keep you in for observation overnight, but I expect to release you tomorrow morning.'

Russ had forbidden Jenny to call him at work, so Martha promised to leave a note on the door of their home so Russ would know where they were.

'I'll be back early tomorrow morning to see how you're doing.' Martha said as she left Jenny's ward.

Mark was sent to the paediatric ward and Jenny to the maternity ward, so they didn't see each other until morning. In the morning, when Dr. Sims asked her how she felt, Jenny smiled and replied, 'I feel fine. I'm surprised that I do, but I feel fine.'

'You can go home, but if you have any further symptoms don't hesitate to call me right away.' he said as he signed her discharge papers. Jenny dressed and wheeled herself to Mark's ward to see how he was doing. The ward nurse stated, 'Dr. Williams says he can be released this morning. He's smiling and waiting for his mommy to come. He'll be glad to see you.'

Jenny cuddled Mark, signed his discharge papers and took him for a ride in her wheelchair back to her ward. Soon Martha arrived and drove them home. When they arrived, Russ was still in bed, but as soon as he heard them in the kitchen he got up.

'How could you do something so careless?' Jenny asked as she pointed to the electrical outlet that now had its proper cover on it. 'How could you be so careless! All of us could have died!'

'I'm sorry. I was in a rush to get to work. I guess I forgot to put it on.' he replied quietly.

Jenny just gave him a scathing look and made coffee for the three of them. Martha had not said a word, but her hostile glance echoed Jenny's comments. She was furious with Russ, didn't trust herself to say a word to him and left shortly after finishing her coffee.

Chapter 17

Three days later, when Russ was doing their weekly shopping, Jenny's water broke and a few minutes later she had her first labour pain. She called Dr Sims who advised her to come directly to the hospital to ward off infection. Jenny promised to do so as soon as Russ returned.

She packed a bag for herself and two for Mark then phoned Martha to ask if she could look after Mark. Martha had already agreed to look after Mark during Jenny's confinement, but this was six weeks earlier than she expected. She agreed, and they dropped Mark off on their way to the hospital. Martha came out of her home and reached for Mark as Russ carried the two bags Jenny had packed for him. Jenny rolled down the car window and Martha reached her free hand through the window and placed it on Jenny's shoulder. 'I'll be thinking about you and rooting for you and the baby. Everything will turn out fine.'

Jenny's labour was long and arduous – far different than when she'd delivered Mark. After thirty-four hours of hard, painful labour, their son Bruce was born. He weighed only five pounds but was considered a big baby seeing he was born six weeks prematurely. Dr. Sims said he would likely have been close to ten-pounds if he'd been born full term.

Because he was a preemie and was having breathing problems he was whisked away and placed in an incubator. Jenny was taken to her room and when she felt a bit rested asked the nurse if she go to the nursery to see her new son.

'We'd like to hold off on that for a while.' said the nurse.

Immediately Jenny began to panic. 'Why won't you let me see my baby? Is something the matter with him?' she asked. Pictures of Thalidomide babies flashed in front of her eyes.

'Oh no – he's fine. Because your water broke, we took the precaution of taking a blood sample to see if you had picked up any infection. Well it appears that you do have an infection and by the look of your left eye,' she said as she examined it, 'You're heading for a bout of conjunctivitis.'

Jenny gave her a questioning look.

'The popular name for that is 'pink eye' and it's highly infectious. You'll have to be in isolation yourself and until we know for sure, we don't want you to go near your baby in case you pass it on to him.'

When Russ visited her that afternoon before going to work, he had to wear a mask. They discussed names for the new baby and decided they would call him Bruce.

Jenny did have conjunctivitis, so was not able to go near Bruce. She was dripping milk, but they couldn't give it to Bruce in case it passed her infection to him. But, they did pump her breasts, so she would continue producing milk. She normally would have gone home the next day, but they were worried that she would pass the conjunctivitis to her family at home.

By the time Jenny was discharged from the hospital four days after her delivery, she had almost stopped producing milk. She was told that Bruce would have to remain in his incubator until his weight returned to five pounds and his breathing improved, so she wouldn't have been able to nurse him anyway.

Russ picked Jenny up at the hospital then retrieved Mark at her parent's home. When Jenny arrived, Mark acted very shy and played strange with her. He even hid under a little throw rug in Martha's hallway. Jenny wondered whether he thought she had deserted him because she was gone so long. He finally let Jenny hug him and Russ drove them home.

That day, Russ as usual, left for work shortly after three, leaving the two of them on their own. Mark was cranky and miserable, which was unusual behaviour for him. Jenny thought he might be overtired so put him to bed early and flopped into her own bed and was soon dead to the world.

The next morning, she was giving Mark his breakfast when she saw something liquid running from his ear. She checked and saw that he had a clear discharge from his ear. 'So that's why he was so cranky!' she thought, 'He's probably got an ear infection.'

She made an appointment with Dr. Williams their paediatrician and Russ drove them to his office. When the doctor examined Mark, he agreed with her prognosis. He also looked carefully at Jenny. 'How are you feeling yourself?' he asked.

'I could be better. I have a sore throat.' she admitted.

He took a quick look at her throat and said, 'You've got a nasty red throat. I wouldn't be surprised if its strep throat. Let me take a swab and see if it is. In the meantime, I want both of you on antibiotics.'

Russ stopped at the drug store to fill their prescriptions and drove them home. They both went to bed and slept and didn't even wake up when Russ went to work. When Russ came home at midnight Jenny woke up. 'How are you feeling?' he asked

'My throat is still sore, and Mark is miserable with his ear infection.' she croaked.

'I hate to tell you this, but I feel awful too. I think I caught something from you two.' he announced.

The next morning Russ went to Dr. Sims and was told he had tonsillitis. So, all three of them were so ill they could hardly manage for the next week. Jenny became the nursemaid for all three of them. She contacted the hospital and let them know how sick they were. The ward head nurse advised them not to come near the hospital to see Bruce until everyone was better.

Finally, when Bruce was three weeks old and she, Mark and Russ were feeling better, Jenny received word that she could bring Bruce home from the hospital. He looked so tiny next to Mark. Mark patted the little bundle and said, 'Baby. Baby.'

'Yes Mark. That's your little brother Bruce. Can you say Bruce?' she enquired.

'Brut.' he said. Mark had been saying words for months and seemed to pick up words very easily. He was also toilet trained and did not wear diapers any more. Jenny thanked her lucky stars that she only had one baby in diapers.

Elaine came over the next afternoon. Russ was lying on the sofa with Bruce on his chest under a baby blanket.

'Well, where is this little darling?' asked Elaine.

'Russ has him.' replied Jenny.

'Where? I don't see any baby?' she said as she gazed at Russ.

Russ pulled back the baby blanket and there on his chest, under the blanket was the little bump that was Bruce.

'Oh my God!' she exclaimed, 'He's so tiny!'

Jenny thought he looked like a little wrinkled baby monkey. He had blonde fuzz all over his cheeks just like peach fuzz. He was adorable. His tiny arms were the size of Russ's thumb and his fingers were miniscule. She'd seen Russ gazing with amazement at the tiny baby with wonderment on his face.

However, Jenny was dismayed that she hadn't been able to bond with Bruce until he was three weeks old. He was a baby who was not comfortable being cuddled and often cried if someone picked him up. Jenny also wondered if the electrical shock had affected him in some way. Dr Sims said it was too early to determine whether he had any permanent brain damage from the shock but would test him when he got older. Jenny was very sad to realise that she did not feel the closeness with Bruce that she'd always felt with Mark and of course could not breast feed him and have that special bond either.

Bruce was a fussy baby but loved his food. Jenny soon learned that when he awoke from his naps, he wanted food – now! One day when she was preparing a meal and Russ and Mark were out in the back yard, she thought she heard Bruce stir in the bedroom. Instead of heating his bottle as she usually did, she went directly to his dimly lit bedroom. He was silent. She looked closer and was alarmed by what she observed. His little face was blue, and his eyes stared at her. She put down the crib side, snatched him up and took him into the living room where there was better light. He wasn't breathing. *Crib death*! she thought in terror.

She screamed for Russ, and began infant resuscitation knowing that she had to be careful not to blow too hard into his little lungs. She also knew that she should cover both his nose and mouth with her mouth. After she had given her first puff of air, she looked at Bruce. He was still not breathing. She did it again. He was still not breathing. By that time Russ and Mark were standing at her side watching what she was doing.

'I've called an ambulance.' Russ said. Their car was in the shop getting repaired, so they had no way of getting him to the hospital.

Thankfully, after her third puff of air, Bruce began breathing and let out a little mewing sound. His face had a puzzled look then he took a big breath and bellowed his rage.

Soon a police car pulled up at the door, lights flashing. The officer said, 'All the ambulances are out right now. We're to take your son to the hospital. How is he?'

Jenny was able to tell the officer that she had done pulmonary resuscitation on Bruce and that he was now breathing all right. The officer peered into Bruce's face and nodded. 'We still should get him to the hospital to see what happened to him.'

When Bruce was admitted, the doctor on call that day said they were lucky - that Bruce would likely have died if Jenny hadn't immediately resuscitated him. 'It could have been a case of SIDS.' he said as he gazed at the parents.

Russ's puzzled look confirmed that he did not know what SIDS was, so he explained, 'Sudden Infant Death Syndrome'. We have no idea what causes some babies to die suddenly and unexplainably. From what you've said, he's a robust, healthy baby. But we'll have to put him into the hospital on a monitor in case the same thing happens again.'

The next day, Bruce's nose was running like a tap. He'd been in the early stages of a bad cold. The doctor said that the cause of his breathing problems was likely a plug of mucus that had settled in his throat as he slept. He advised Jenny to place him on his side when he slept to ensure he didn't have the same problem again. He did however want to keep Bruce in the hospital for two more days on the monitor in case he stopped breathing again.

Bruce went home on the fourth day and was fine except for his runny nose. He never had another episode like that again.

Chapter 18

When Bruce was eighteen months old Russ purchased a piece of property on the waterfront at Sunset Beach, fifty miles from Winnipeg. It was close to Grand Beach where Jenny had spent most of her childhood summers. Jenny didn't know until later that Russ had the property and the cottage they later constructed together listed in his name only. The property was lakefront, but when they first saw it, it was covered by trees and brush. By now, Jenny was out of her wheel chair, used a cane to walk and was able to drive a car. Her balance was still not perfect, but she managed quite well without her wheelchair.

Russ and Jenny spent every weekend clearing the lot by hand while Jenny's sister Susan babysat the boys. Russ cut the wood into eighteen-inch pieces to use later as firewood. The rest of the brush and debris he took to the dump. In town Russ was able to find an old house that a contractor wanted torn down. In exchange, Russ could keep all the lumber from the building. He made several trips down to the beach property to deliver the wood. However, he realised that he would need many supplies before he could start to build their cottage.

'Where are we going to find the money to buy roof rafters and trusses, shingles, nails and other things I don't have?' Russ asked Jenny.

'We don't have much in our savings account, do we?' she replied.

'I wonder if we could borrow some money from your parents? I'll get my Christmas bonus in December, so we could pay them back then.' suggested Russ.

'I can ask them, but they may say 'no'.' Jenny said cautiously.

Jenny spoke with Ian and Martha who agreed to lend them the fifteen hundred dollars Russ estimated they would need to start building their cottage. When Russ got his

Christmas bonus, he spent it on more material to add inside walls to the cottage but never repaid her parents for the money that was borrowed.

After two years, the cottage was completed sufficiently enough that they spent many happy weekends and summers there. The boys enjoyed playing on the beach in front of their cottage. They built sandcastles and swam in the water and thoroughly enjoyed the short Canadian summers. They frequently saw white pelicans that roosted on a nearby island. Russ built a dock in front of their cottage and bought a small rowboat, so they could enjoy the occasional boat ride.

Because of her lifeguard training Jenny insisted that they all wear life jackets when they were in any boat. She remembered the story she'd been told when she took her lifeguard training about a man who had taken his twelve-year-old son and eight-year-old daughter on a boat trip. Both children wore life jackets, but the father did not. They hit a log and the father was thrown from the boat. He hid his head and was unconscious and started sinking. His son tried to save him but couldn't go down to save his father because of his life jacket, so he took it off and dove down after his father. He never surfaced. The eight-year-old daughter was left alone in the boat for over an hour before another boat came along and rescued her. She was traumatized for months. Because of that Jenny insisted that all people in a boat wear life jackets - whether they were adults or children.

They were able to purchase an old wood-burning stove for the cottage from a farmer. This had been Russ's reason for cutting up all the timber he found on the property when he was clearing it. The stove had a big water container on the side that provided plenty of hot water needed for bathing or washing up and a warming rack where food could be kept warm while the rest of the meal was cooking. It was also instrumental in keeping the cottage warm on cooler days.

Everyone agreed that food cooked on it seemed to taste better somehow than those cooked on the electric stove at home. The smell of Jenny cooking bacon and eggs on the stove with toast being kept warm on the warming shelf would be the family's occasional welcome to the day. One of their favourite treats was when one of the local fishermen came to the door selling fresh pickerel that tasted especially good when fried in butter over the wood stove. They enjoyed many evenings gathered around the old wooden table. The boys made puzzles while their parents did their evening chores.

Russ often suffered from poison ivy that would leave him with ugly watery sores on his body that itched terribly. One weekend when he was having a bout of it, he was working inside the cabin installing a large plate glass picture window in the front of their cottage that overlooked the lake. He had just secured the window with several huge spikes per side when they heard a radio announcer say there was a storm coming their way across the lake. Lake Winnipeg could be a dangerous lake and had been for thousands of years. Sailors knew they had to carefully check the weather patterns before venturing out any distance from shore. Winds and squalls could materialise in minutes and make it a bubbling cauldron. The announcer warned people living on their side of the lake that the storm would likely push large amounts of water their way and to expect some flooding in low-lying areas. That meant the storm was heading right towards them.

They looked outside and saw nothing but a beautiful sunny day. However, they knew from stories they'd heard about the lake that they needed to heed such warnings.

Because Russ was suffering from poison ivy and dared not get wet, they decided that he should concentrate on securing the picture window, so it would withstand the storm.

'I'd better let our neighbours know that the storm is coming,' said Jenny as she headed out the door. After warning their neighbours, Jenny and the boys put anything outside that could possibly blow or be swept away into a little shed at the side of their cottage. When Jenny glanced around the yard to make sure she'd removed everything, she spotted their car parked at the end of their property. Making sure the boys were safe in the cabin, she grabbed the keys and moved their car to a road two blocks away on higher ground. By the time she walked back to the cottage, ugly storm clouds had formed over the lake and it was obvious that the storm was heading their way.

She and Russ watched in horror through the temporarily secured picture window, as a dark line formed across the lake. The line kept coming towards their cottage. As it got closer and closer, they realised that it was a huge wall of water and it was obviously going to hit their cottage. Their cottage was built about one hundred yards from the water, but a slope raised it about ten feet above the waterline. The cottage sat on twenty-four piers that were made of four eighteen-inch square hollow concrete blocks, piled one on top of the other. In the middle of those blocks were pieces of telephone poles that had been driven into the ground that kept the blocks from moving.

Jenny quickly handed out life jackets and helped the boys secure theirs. When the wave hit the cottage, it was high enough that it hit the bottom of the newly placed front window and water gushed in around the sides, soaking everything in the area.

They scurried back from the window praying that the big spikes would hold the huge piece of glass against the onslaught. Suddenly they heard a terrible thumping and banging under their cottage and wondered if it was going to collapse into the water and possibly float away with them in it. They huddled together at the back of the cottage, the boys wide-eyed with wonder as the big wave hit their cottage. They peered out the window in the back door and saw that the wave had gone as far as the road and a bit beyond. Their car could possibly have floated away if Jenny had not moved it.

Soon the banging stopped, and they were relieved to see that their cottage remained upright. The water receded, taking with it anything that was not secured – bushes, small trees, sand and mud. The area around the cottage was a sea of mud and debris. Their dock had disappeared except for the occasional big rock that had been under it.

When the storm passed, Russ went out to survey the area under the cottage. He saw that the banging they'd heard had been caused by a full-length telephone pole that had banged again and again against some of the piers. After the storm, the pole was half submerged under the cottage in sand and mud and nine of the twenty-four piers were damaged or gone. Thankfully, the missing piers were scattered, so the cottage was not in danger of collapsing. What a mess!

It took Russ two of his weekends to remove portions of the telephone pole with a chain saw. First, he had to dig around it, prop the huge telephone pole up with bricks then use a chain saw to cut it into moveable pieces. With little more than three feet to work under the floorboards of the cabin, it was dangerous work. Then he tackled the repair of the concrete piers. He and Hugh Mackenzie rented huge house jacks that held the cottage up while they replaced the damaged piers. Those weekends Jenny and the boys stayed home because the dangerous job they were doing required that the cottage to be vacant. He then cleared the lot of debris and replaced their boat dock.

Chapter 19

Eighteen months after Bruce's birth Jenny became pregnant again – this time they hoped it would be a girl. Now they really needed a newer home and began searching for a bargain. They were able to find a lovely bungalow that had three bedrooms and an unfinished basement.

Russ got busy refinishing the basement. He divided it into a rumpus room, a workroom and a laundry room. When the walls were completed, Russ built a huge train set layout in the rumpus room. Russ bought expensive train sets and built an elaborate setup including towns, mountains and lakes. It kept the boys entertained, but they weren't allowed to touch the set – only Russ could do that. Over the next few years, Russ added more train track to the already huge train extravaganza.

Jenny's pregnancy was normal, no morning sickness this time, and she felt very healthy. Then suddenly, in early November, when she was seven and a half months pregnant, her water broke, and she was rushed to the hospital. This labour lasted thirty-eight hours and Jenny cried when she was told that her baby – a boy had died shortly after his birth. Jenny went home from the hospital with empty arms and for weeks suffered from post partum depression. She cried and cried but had two toddlers to care for so forced herself to get through the days. Russ was no help and simply told her to 'get over it.'

She was still bleeding quite heavily when she went for her six-week check-up with Dr. Sims. When she explained about the bleeding, he frowned and pressed her abdomen then said, 'I want to do an internal examination.'

After he examined her, he stated, 'I want you to have an X-ray taken of your abdomen. I can feel a mass near your left ovary and need to check to see what it is.'

He sent her to an X-ray clinic where she had several X-rays taken. She was dismayed to learn that she would not have the results until the next day when she was to see Dr. Sims again. She sat shaking as she waited for the results.

'You have a mass attached to your left ovary. We think it could have been growing throughout your pregnancy. We'll have to remove it, but because you're still haemorrhaging, I want you to be in better physical health before we can remove it. I will book the surgery for mid-January. In the meantime, I want you to take it easy and try to gain some weight. You're far too thin right now, and I want you to eat lots during the Christmas holidays.'

'How big is the lump and what do you think the lump is?' she asked fearfully.

'The lump is the size of a grapefruit. We're not sure what it is because we don't know how long it's been growing inside you. It could be a benign cyst or tumour. The worst-case scenario is that it's malignant. However, I doubt that it is.'

Jenny left his office feeling defeated, depressed and worried about the next crisis she'd have to face. Hadn't she had enough problems in her life? Life wasn't fair. When she got home she wondered how she could prepare for the fact that she could possibly be dying - dying of cancer. She'd learned that ovarian cancer was one of the deadliest cancers - and she possibly had it.

What steps did one take to prepare for such an eventuality? Should she prepare for a burial plot? Should she make out a will? Should she clean out all the unnecessary stuff she had accumulated, but didn't need? What was one expected to do when one could possibly have a limited time to live? In the end, she did nothing as she slipped into an even deeper depression.

When she told her parents, they were naturally concerned. Martha helped with Mark and Bruce as much as she could, and Russ made stabs at doing some of the housework. They were all worried because Jenny spent much of her time moping about, just staring into space or reading a book. It was a terrible Christmas for everyone as they contemplated whether Jenny did or did not have cancer. Jenny lost even more weight. Although she tried, she couldn't seem to gain weight and looked very haggard and pale in pictures taken during the holiday season.

She entered the hospital the afternoon of January 15th and the surgery was performed the next day. The morning of the surgery, her parents came to see her before she was wheeled into surgery. Russ was at home with the boys.

'Mom, if it is cancer – who will look after the boys? You know Russ is hopeless with them. And if I die, how will they be brought up?'

'I want you to go into your surgery thinking positively. Tell yourself – you do *not* have cancer. If the worst happens, you know we'll always be around to help out.' Martha said as Jenny was wheeled into an elevator. Jenny waved then laid back on the stretcher, tears streaming down her face.

Martha and Ian sat waiting for their daughter to return from surgery. Both were terrified that Jenny's concerns could in fact be true. What would Russ do if Jenny died? Would he ignore his sons as he did now? Would he realise that he couldn't manage them and let them bring up the children? Would he give the children up for adoption? Martha felt sick thinking of what might happen to her lovely grandsons.

Jenny awoke from surgery with a scar eight inches long that started from her mid abdomen downward. Dr. Sims had good news for her, 'The lump was a benign cyst, but we had to remove your left ovary.'

They all breathed a sigh of relief. However, it took Jenny several months to recover from losing her baby and from her surgery. One of the reasons she found it so difficult to recover was Russ's attitude when he saw how deeply depressed she was.

'Stop feeling sorry for yourself and get on with life!' were his comments. More and more, Jenny realised that Russ did not seem capable of showing empathy for her or anyone else, nor did he give her the sympathy and support she needed so desperately.

She had just recovered from her surgery when three months later, on April Fool's Day, Jenny heard Russ as he came home from work. He was making a lot of thumping noises and when she looked at her bedside clock, saw it was three o'clock. Her immediate thought was that Russ had been drinking but when she investigated, she learned that the noise was caused by the crutches he was using.

'What happened?' she asked as she tied a housecoat around her.

'I injured my knee at work. They took me to the emergency department for X-rays and the doctor has booked me to have my cartilage removed in two day's time.' he replied as he sat down carefully on a kitchen chair – his damaged leg straight out in front of him.

There was no such thing in those days as keyhole surgery - so he had major surgery. At the hospital, before he underwent surgery, he reached for Jenny's hand and she became aware that he was terrified and needed her support. He explained that the only time he'd been in the hospital was when he'd had his tonsils out when he was a child, and he was afraid he would die on the operating table. Jenny couldn't help but wonder why he didn't understand the kind of terror she'd felt when she was going through the trauma or her car accident and during her disastrous pregnancies. Could he not equate his terror with what she'd already endured in her short life?

Russ came through the surgery well and was on crutches but unable to work for six weeks. It had been seven years since she'd had her accident and thankfully she could now walk without a cane or assistance. Jenny cared for him and her sons and tried to recover mentally herself.

Chapter 20

Russ had just returned to work after his knee surgery when Russ's mother, Nellie phoned to ask if she could come over to speak with Jenny. Nellie lived with Antonio in the home she'd shared with Frank before his death. Jenny wondered what her mother-in-law wanted to discuss. When Nellie arrived, she took Jenny into her bedroom and said, 'I have something I need to discuss with you. I can't talk to Antonio or Russ, because they likely wouldn't know what to advise me.'

Jenny nodded, 'Please tell me what's concerning you.'

'I have a rash on my left breast that I want you to look at. I've had it for three weeks and it's just getting worse. It's so tender and itchy and I can't seem to stop scratching it.' she said worriedly.

Jenny watched as her mother-in-law shyly exposed her breasts. The woman was so shy that Jenny knew that this must be an ordeal for her. Jenny peered carefully at the rash. It was very red and inflamed and when she touched the skin it felt very hot and looked swollen.

'I also have a lump under that arm.' Nellie added almost as an afterthought.

'This is definitely something that your doctor should examine. Why don't you phone and see whether he can see you today?' suggested Jenny.

Nellie phoned and was able to see her general practitioner, Dr. McNeil that afternoon. Because Nellie couldn't drive and didn't have a car, Jenny drove her in her old car. Nellie's doctor sent her to a clinic that was down the hall from his office to have a mammogram.

'Please return to Dr. McNeil's office and I'll send him the results.' advised the X-ray technician after she'd completed the mammogram.

When Dr. McNeil beckoned Nellie to come into her office, Nellie asked Jenny if she would come with her. Dr. McNeil looked grim.

'I have bad news. We've detected a large lump in your left breast and another under your left arm. We'll have to surgically remove them. We're almost sure that they're malignant but won't know for sure until we do a biopsy during the surgery. In any case the lumps must be removed. Whether we do a lumpectomy, or a mastectomy depends on what the biopsy shows when we operate.'

Nellie reached for Jenny's hand, became very pale and looked as if she were going to pass out. Dr. McNeil gave her a glass of water and she seemed to rally. 'When do you want to do the operation?' she finally gasped out.

'I'll see what I can arrange. It's possible that what you have could be inflammatory breast disease. It's a fast-moving malignancy, so I want to deal with this as soon as possible. Wait here while I contact the hospital.'

Jenny knelt on the carpet at Nellie's feet and gave her a big hug. Nellie finally allowed herself to cry – sobbing almost as if she were in pain and finally took a large breath to enable her to retain her control. 'I'm so afraid, so afraid.' she gasped.

'I know you are,' consoled Jenny, 'but Russ, Antonio and I will help you through this.'

Dr McNeil returned and said, 'I was able to schedule your surgery for a week tomorrow. You'll be admitted to the hospital late Tuesday afternoon and the surgery will be done early Wednesday morning.'

Jenny drove her home. Antonio was now home from work and immediately noticed how upset Nellie was. He asked, 'What's wrong Mom?'

Nelly and Jenny explained what had happened. Antonio just sat there with an agonised look on his face. His mother had always been so healthy. This was the first time he could recall her having anything more than a cold or the flu. When Jenny told Russ the news, he was just as stunned and surprised as his brother. They'd both lost their father to cancer, and now their mother could possibly die of the same horrible illness.

That next week Nellie had her operation. Mid-way through the operation, they had to wait for the pathology department to analyse the biopsy they'd taken. Dr. McNeil shook his head at the terrible analysis that it was indeed a malignant tumour and proceeded to perform a mastectomy and removed the lymph glands under her left arm.

Jenny was at home with the children when Dr McNeil called her to tell her that it was cancer and that he'd had to remove her breast and lymph glands. He also explained that Nellie was coming out of the anaesthetic but kept insisting that she had to go home to cook supper for her husband. She was delirious and was in danger of ripping her stitches as she kept trying to pull herself up in her bed and climb over the bed railings. He asked Jenny if she could possibly come and try to calm her down.

Jenny dropped the boys at Martha's and rushed to the ICU ward. When she arrived, she saw that the hospital had put restraining ties on her mother-in-law's wrists, so she couldn't climb out of her bed. Nellie seemed to be awake but had a wild look in her eyes. Jenny went over to her and said in as calm a voice as she could, 'Hi Mom. It's Jenny. How are you feeling?'

'Got to make Frank's dinner!' she shouted.

'No Mom. You're in the hospital. You've just had an operation. Do you remember?' she asked anxiously.

Nellie looked at her and the veil of memory loss lifted 'Yes. Hi Jenny. How long have you been there?'

'I just arrived, Mom. The hospital called me because you were trying to climb over the railings. You insisted that you had to go home to make dinner for Frank.' she explained.

'I must have been out of it then.' she said as she glanced at the restraints. 'You can remove these now.'

Jenny nodded to the nurse who removed the restraints.

'Mom, the best thing for you to do now, is to sleep. You've just come out of the anaesthetic so need to rest so you can recover.' Jenny advised.

'Yes, I do feel tired.' Nellie admitted as she smiled at Jenny. 'Thanks for coming. Where are the children?'

'They're at my Mom's place.'

'Well you go to them. I'll be fine now. Antonio will be up to see me as soon as he finishes work. You go home now.' she said as she drifted off.

Nellie had not asked Jenny whether it was cancer or not, so she was glad she didn't have to be the one to tell her.

A week later, when Nellie was well enough to be discharged from the hospital it was obvious that she couldn't go to her own home. Antonio would be at work all day and Nellie was not well enough to look after herself. So Russ and Jenny took her to their home and made her comfortable.

One of the hardest things Jenny had to do while she cared for Nellie was to bathe her. Nellie insisted that she wanted to take a tub bath. She was a short but large woman and had difficulty getting in and out of their bathtub without assistance. Because her surgery included removal of the lymph nodes under her left breast, Jenny couldn't help her in and out by lifting that arm. Besides with her own weak back, she couldn't even contemplate lifting the woman. So, with much physical effort, Nellie was finally able to hoist herself out of the tub. Jenny vowed not to let her have another tub bath again until her surgical area was healed.

Nellie had been there a week when she asked, 'Jenny, would you look at this for me?' and pointed to a small lump on her left arm between her elbow and shoulder.

'I think it's something your doctor should see.' replied Jenny. 'Do you want me to phone him and see if he can see you?'

'Yes, I guess I should see about it in case it is infection caused by my surgery.'

Russ was at home and was able to drive Nellie to see her doctor just after lunch. He was very upset when he phoned Jenny a short time later. 'I had just taken Mom into the doctor's office when she had a heart attack! The doctor revived her, and she's been taken to the hospital in an ambulance. I'm there now and will go directly to work from here.'

Three days later, shortly before Christmas, Nellie had a massive stroke and lapsed into a coma. Jenny, Russ and Antonio went up to see her. They stared down at her knowing how seriously ill she was.

'What if she dies?' asked Antonio.

'Has she bought a funeral plot next to Dad's?' Russ asked.

Jenny looked at them and pointed to the hallway. When they were outside the door she said, 'You do realise don't you, that even though your mother's in a coma, she might still be able to hear everything you say? So, watch what you say when you're near her.'

The men were obviously not aware of this and felt terrible that they'd said something like that in her presence. They decided they would go to the hospital cafeteria to have a cup of coffee. Jenny returned to her mother-in-law's room. She was sitting beside Nellie when she noticed that the woman was pulling away at her covers with her hands. Jenny, an avid reader of body language thought she understood what Nellie was trying to tell her. 'Mom, it's Jenny. Do you want a bedpan?'

The woman's hands stopped pulling at the covers.

'Hold on a minute Mom. I'll get a nurse to help you.'

Jenny went to get a nurse and both of them helped put Nellie onto a bedpan. Nellie passed her water even though she was still mainly in a coma.

Unfortunately, the next day Nellie had another massive stroke and passed away in December 1965.

Something Missing

122

Chapter 21

Nellie was buried in the plot next to Frank. Reverend Thompson officiated at the service. Mark and Bruce stayed with Martha while their parents were at the funeral. Jenny felt they were far too young to come to the funeral.

After Nellie's funeral, family and friends came back to Russ and Jenny's home for refreshments. Later most of their friends left giving their condolences and only Hugh Mackenzie, Antonio, Jenny and Russ remained.

Hugh had been very close to Nellie and had taken her death very hard. He opened a bottle of Johnny Walker whisky and started filling everyone's glasses. Jenny held her hand over her glass. She didn't feel like drinking hard liquor, so left the men to mourn. Soon Antonio, Russ and Hugh were feeling no pain.

Jenny was busy washing dishes in the kitchen when she felt someone's arms encircle her waist and felt the person nuzzling her neck. She suddenly realised that this person was several inches shorter than Russ. She glanced around and saw that it was Hugh nuzzling her. 'What are you doing?' she exclaimed.

'I've wanted you ever since I first saw you,' he murmured.

She turned and pushed him away. 'How could you do this to your best friend when he's just buried his mother?'

Hugh sheepishly turned around and left the kitchen. *What got into him?* Jenny wondered, then realised that it was likely the booze talking.

The next day Russ was at work when their doorbell rang. It was Hugh. *I guess he's going to apologise.* she thought as she beckoned him to come in.

'I just had to see you again.' he started, 'Not to apologise for what I did, but to tell you again that I meant it.

I'm crazy about you and have been for years. And I know Russ doesn't treat you very well.'

Jenny remembered how attracted she had been to him before she'd married Russ so her next comments were painful for her to speak, 'Well Hugh, both of us are married now and you know Doreen and I are close friends. This can't happen and we're both going to have to forget you ever discussed this with me.' she said as her heart pounded.

'Are you sure?' he asked.

'Dead sure.' she replied as she ushered him to the door.

When the door closed behind him she thought, *Why, oh why didn't he tell me that before I married Russ?*

Any time she saw Hugh thereafter she felt a twinge of guilt, but knew she'd handled the situation the only way she could have. Her friendship with Doreen was as strong as ever.

Chapter 22

It was only a short time after Nellie's death that Antonio realised that he was lonely and had nobody to look after him. He had paid Russ half of what he and Russ had considered his parent's home was worth and decided to continue living in his parent's former home. He solved his loneliness problem by asking Jean Church, a co-worker to marry him. They had dated for several months and seemed to get along very well.

Jean's lease for her apartment ended two months before their wedding, so Jenny and Russ offered to let her move into their spare bedroom until their marriage. One night shortly after the adults had gone to bed, Jean heard a loud crash coming from across the hall. She dashed out of her bed but was relieved then heard both Jenny and Russ laughing uproariously. She stepped across the hallway and tapped on their bedroom door.

'May I come in?' she asked.

'Come in.' laughed Jenny.

When Jean entered the room, it became clear what had caused the loud bang and why Jenny and Russ were laughing so hard. Their bed did not have a box spring under the mattress. Instead it had a metal railing firmly attached to the headboard. Across the metal railing were many six-inch boards that supported the mattress. Because this made the bed lower off the floor, it was easier for Jenny to get into and out of bed. Somehow the boards had shifted as Russ climbed into bed that night causing their bed to collapse. Jenny had been catapulted onto Russ's side of the bed and if he hadn't caught her, she would have been flung onto the floor.

What made them laugh so hard was that as the bed fell to the floor, Russ's shoulder had jarred the tall dresser on his side of the bed. That had caused an empty musical liquor bottle sitting on top of it to fall over. As Jean entered their room, it was still gaily playing 'For he's a jolly good fellow' and she too started to laugh.

Jean hurried over to help Jenny out of bed and Russ rolled out of the bed shortly afterwards. He lifted the mattress up and asked Jenny to hold it while he and Jean replaced the slats on the metal railing. Then he replaced the mattress and they all helped re-make the bed.

The next morning, they were still laughing about how ironic it was that the music that played was so appropriate at the time of the situation.

Because Jean's family lived in a small town in Saskatchewan, they decided to celebrate their wedding there. Antonio asked Russ to be his best man at the wedding. Jenny got busy making little jackets for the boys and a pretty dress for herself. They had fun at the wedding, and Russ was more romantic towards Jenny, nuzzling her neck while he danced and took more time than usual when he made love to her that evening.

In March of that year, Winnipeg had what was to become known as 'The March 1966 storm.' Snow started coming down and it kept coming down until it was up to the rooftops of many homes. The temperature in Winnipeg did not go above zero for ninety days. Snow started falling after midnight on Thursday and despite the heavy snow, on Friday morning March 4, people still went to work. By mid-morning the streets were impassable. That morning the busses were called in and were not returned to the streets until the next Saturday morning.

Schools closed on Friday as did stores, restaurants and theatres. The big storm piled up more than fourteen inches of snow that was driven by winds gusting up to seventy miles an hour. Snowmobiles were confiscated or volunteered to the police and volunteers used them to take people to hospitals and to deliver drugs to patients. CB radios were used for the first time to create an emergency communications network. Because the busses were pulled off the streets, those who could not walk home were stuck wherever they were. Thousands of people were stranded at City Hall, eleven hundred staff and customers took refuge at The Bay and sixteen hundred were housed at Eaton's. Because Antonio Worked at Eaton's, he was one of those stranded people. Thankfully the large department stores had restaurants, bedding and blankets that were used for several days by stranded employees and customers.

Because Wednesday and Thursday were Russ's days off, he was at home when the storm hit. They couldn't see out of their kitchen windows and couldn't open their front or back doors because of the snow. Two doors away, a neighbour, Sarah Yellan, had been home from the hospital just a week with a new baby. Her husband was an air traffic controller at the airport and was stranded there, so Sarah was alone with her two children and began to panic. She was not able to nurse her baby and was quickly running out of milk to feed him. In a panic, she phoned Jenny to see if she could somehow get some milk to her.

'Can you open any of your doors?' Jenny asked.

'Yes, the back door was protected by the wind and I can get out that door but can't leave my babies. Eddie's at work and can't get home and I understand that all the stores are closed.'

'We'll do our best to get some milk to you. I have about two quarts here and some powdered milk that you could mix up if the storm lasts too long. I'll phone you when we figure out a way to get the milk to you.'

Jenny and Russ discussed how they could make it happen. Russ started by removing the glass and screen from their side door and began a bucket brigade with the boys to put the snow into their bathtub. After half an hour he was able to remove enough snow, so he could open the door. However, no matter how he tried, he could not climb up to the top of the snow, so he could navigate across the top of the snow. A ladder would have helped, but their ladder was in the garage buried behind mountains of snow.

'If you push me up, I can get to the top. I think I should go.' said Jenny.

'No, I should go, if I can find some way to get up to the top of the snow.' replied Russ.

Mark bravely volunteered to do it, but they knew it would be far too dangerous for him to attempt. Jenny felt that Russ would be far too heavy to crawl over the snow as she planned to do. She knew how dangerous this would be because the snow was so deep, and she could fall through and be trapped with no way to get out. Russ reluctantly agreed that Jenny should be the one to go but they agreed that if she hadn't got to Sarah's within twenty minutes, he would come after her.

By mid-afternoon, the snow had finally stopped falling. Jenny donned her ski jacket, pants and mitts, put a toque on her head and wrapped a scarf around her head. She put the milk into a back pack, so it would be out of the way and wouldn't hamper the use of her hands and feet. It was a bright sunny day that normally would have been a joy to anyone who viewed it, but to Jenny, it could mean life or death.

Russ called Sarah to tell her Jenny was on her way then boosted her up until she was on top of the snow by their back door. She began the slow crawl that resembled doing the breast stroke over the one hundred and twenty feet to Sarah's home. Twice, Jenny started to fall through the snow, but she flattened herself and slowly inched her body forward along the snow. She kept raising her head to see how much progress she was making. It seemed so odd to be able to look at her next-door neighbour's home and realise that she was crawling along at the height of their kitchen windows. It was painstakingly slow progress. Then she spotted the side of Sarah's home. And yes, there was an opening along the side of the house where the snow had barely drifted. She reached that slope and slid down the remaining ten feet to Sarah's back door and stood there brushing the snow that covered her.

Twenty minutes after she had left her home, a very relieved Sarah welcomed Jenny and helped her take off her snow-covered garments. 'I can't thank you enough for doing this dangerous thing for me. I'll never forget this!' she said as she hugged Jenny.

'I'll phone Russ, otherwise he'll panic and start after me.' Jenny said.

'I'll rest a bit then I'll come home. I'll phone you just before I leave.' she informed Russ.

Sarah gave Jenny the cup of tea she'd prepared for her. Then she poured some milk into a bottle and heated it for her infant.

They visited a while then Jenny redressed in her snow gear. Sarah brought a ladder from her basement, donned a jacket herself and Jenny climbed onto the snow again. Sarah became covered with snow herself as Jenny struggled to get traction at the top of the snow. She waved goodbye as she started her crawl home. Sarah brushed herself off and went back into her home.

Jenny didn't follow her original trail but crawled beside the marks she'd made on her initial trip. She laughed when she examined her original trail. It looked as if a lumbering turtle had crawled over the snow. It was a great relief when she arrived safely at her home.

The city was locked down for ten days. Sarah's husband Eddie was able to make it home on one of the volunteered snowmobiles two days later. He arrived with four quarts of milk, so their baby had the nourishment he required.

Chapter 23

Two years after she delivered and lost her baby boy, she and Russ decided to try again to have the daughter they wanted. Jenny didn't know whether she could conceive with only one ovary but tried anyway. When she did conceive, her pregnancy progressed normally.

As they did every year, she and the children went to their cottage at the lake for the summer. Russ came down on his days off, but otherwise she was there alone with the children. Mark was six and Bruce was four and a half that summer and Jenny was five months pregnant. The boys were playing on the beach and Jenny was washing some vegetables in a bucket of rainwater at the front of the cottage when she heard Mark shouting to her. 'Mom come quick - hurry. Bruce fell off the dock and he's stuck under it. Come quick!'

Jenny had forbidden them to go on the dock and was dismayed that they had done so. She ran down the dock as quickly as she could manage and could hear Bruce's voice calling for her under her feet. She jumped into the shallow water beside the dock and swam back a few feet until she could see Bruce's face through the girders. There were high waves that day and he was being swamped by wave after wave that was pushing him closer to shore leaving him less room to breathe under the dock. She poked her hand through the wooden girders at the side of the dock and grabbed Bruce's hand. 'Take a breath honey – here comes another wave.' she shouted.

He did what he was told then as she held one of his arms she told him to move along towards the far end of the dock. Mark patrolled the dock, encouraging them along. Bit by bit, between huge mouthfuls of air as the waves battered him, Bruce moved towards the area where he could escape from under the dock. It seemed to take an eternity but must have been only about ten minutes. Finally, Jenny was able to find a break in the boards at the side of the dock. She scooped Bruce's other hand, lifted him up and cuddled him against her shoulder. He was safe. She could feel his little heart thumping almost as hard as was her own. He held on tight as she walked with him back to the shore and dried him with a towel.

In November, two months later, as had happened twice in her pregnancies before, Jenny's water broke, and she went into early labour. With one and a half months left in her pregnancy, she had hopes that the baby would live. Her labour went on and on and after thirty-eight hours of labour, Dr. Sims finally did an internal examination and announced that the baby was presenting buttocks first – was a breach baby. He turned the baby, and their long-awaited daughter was born. Tragedy struck again, and the daughter she'd named Darla survived only for a few hours. The hardest thing for Jenny to accept was the knowledge that the baby would likely have survived, had the hospital staff identified that hers was a breach birth. Because it was a live birth, they had a funeral and buried little Darla in a small casket beside her Grandmother.

Jenny didn't know until he was an adult and he talked to her about it, that Bruce believed he was responsible for the loss of that baby. How sad that he spent all those years worrying that he was the cause of the baby's death.

Jenny fell into another deep depression, but after a short mourning period, she and Russ realised that they couldn't go through the trauma of another pregnancy. Because Jenny still ached for a daughter, they decided to adopt a baby girl. In mid-December, just six weeks after she had lost her last baby, they completed the paperwork to put their name on the list of many parents wanting to adopt a baby. They expected it to be a couple of years before a baby would be available.

Both were thrilled, excited and overwhelmed when in mid-February, only two months after signing the papers, they were presented with their beautiful eleven-day-old adopted daughter they named Debbie. Her parents were university students who knew it would be better for Debbie if they gave her up. When Jenny first saw Debbie, she couldn't believe that her parents had agreed to give her up, especially if they had seen her before doing so. Debbie was a beautiful baby, with big brown eyes, adorable cupid-bow lips and tiny nose. Jenny was content. Her family was complete.

Throughout the years, Debbie continued to be beautiful, but the best thing about her beauty was that she didn't seem to know how attractive she was. She remained self-conscious, never realising the affect she had on any red-blooded male who saw her. When she was a teenager she was stunningly beautiful and turned heads wherever she went.

Chapter 24

When Mark was eight and Bruce was almost seven, Jenny registered them in pee-wee hockey. The only time the instructors could get inside ice time was at six-thirty in the morning on Tuesday and Saturday mornings. Because Russ didn't arrive home the night before until about twelve forty-five, they decided that Russ should stay home with Debbie. They both normally slept until Jenny and the boys returned from the skating rink.

It was Jenny's job to get the boys up early enough to feed, dress and drive them to the rink for their lessons. What a chore it was getting them dressed! By the time she had one fully dressed in his hockey paraphernalia that included shin pads, elbow pads, kidney pads, hockey socks, shirts, helmets and pants, she had to tackle the second. By the time the second one was dressed, the first one had to go to the bathroom. It would have been rather funny if it hadn't been so early in the morning.

When she got them to the arena, more fun began as she laced them into their hockey skates. They fell down so often she was glad they had so much protective gear and padding. Their coach Darren Stewart was a big bear of a man who had five children of his own – two of them boys. He had infinite patience with these bundled up little Stanley Cup hopefuls. Jenny realised that at the end of the sessions, he must have had a sore back because of the number of times he had to pick the many young boys off the ice. For several winters Jenny shared hot cups of coffee with the other mothers and thoroughly enjoyed the chance to communicate with others.

A beautiful ornamental crab apple tree grew in Jenny's front yard. It had grown over the years until it was now over thirty feet high and displayed the most beautiful blossoms in May. It produced tiny little apples that Jenny used to make pies and crab apple wine. One year at the end of autumn, some apples had remained at the top of the tree. These became frozen over the winter, then when spring came, the heat caused them to ferment.

One Saturday morning, Mark came running into the house with several other neighbourhood children close behind, 'Mom, come quick! There are birds all over the place and they're acting funny!'

Jenny looked in amazement as several Bohemian Waxwing birds staggered and fell over on her lawn. Some were still eating the apples and she realised they were all drunk from the fermented fruit. 'Go get some those empty shoe boxes I put in the basement.' she said to Mark. 'The rest of you kids go home and see if you can find any small boxes with a lid too.'

Jenny punched holes in the top of the boxes. The children gently collected the birds and put them in the boxes lined with face cloths, so they could sleep it off. A male neighbour brought over a long ladder and knocked all the remaining apples to the ground. The children laughed as they ran around collecting the apples, so the birds would not be able to eat any more of them and act 'silly.' They took turns guarding their drunk patients from cats and other predators and as they recovered they let them go.

When Debbie was fifteen months old, Jenny had to curtail taking the boys to their hockey practices. Debbie had just awakened from her afternoon nap and Jenny had knelt on the bathroom floor to place her on her little potty. Suddenly she felt a sharp knife-like pain in her right knee. She cried out in pain. Debbie looked at her and started to howl herself.

Jenny tried to push herself sideways off her knees, but it just sent shards of pain shooting through her right knee when she tried to do so. She called for Bruce and he looked worriedly at her as he noticed the tears of pain on her face.

'Mommy has hurt her knee. I need you to gently push me over that way, so I can get off my knees.' she instructed.

Bruce sent a questioning look at her, hesitated for a moment then did as she asked. When Jenny was off her knees, she was able to scoot herself along the hall on her bottom until she reached the phone. Ironically, it was April the first, two years to the day after Russ had damaged the cartilage in his knee.

Then it was Jenny's turn to be on crutches, but there was little help from Russ. Her mother came over in the evenings when Russ was at work to make dinner and put the children to bed then went back home. Jenny's surgery had complications and several weeks after her surgery it became obvious that she couldn't straighten her injured knee properly. A set of X-rays revealed that the surgeon had inadvertently left in a piece of cartilage at the back of her knee, so she had to undergo further surgery. This kept her on crutches for another six weeks, so she was unable to walk properly for a total of three months.

Chapter 25

While she was incapacitated, Jenny had a chance to think about her life and realised that there was something drastically missing in it. Often, she felt alone and so lonely she felt like weeping. She became so depressed that at one point she contemplated suicide.

Did she love Russ? Had she ever loved Russ, or had it been a girlhood fantasy that she was in love with him? Would she have chosen Russ as a husband if she had not been so young and naïve? Now that she was twenty-eight, would she have chosen him as a husband?

What did love mean? What did it involve? Shouldn't love mean that you felt so close to another person that you'd do everything in your power to make your life with them a good one? Did Russ do that for her? Did she do that for him? Jenny felt in her heart that she had done her part in the marriage, but had Russ done his?

What she missed the most was the emotional and mental stimulation of having adult conversations with others. Russ was hopeless in this area – often eating his dinner in silence. He would then go down to his workshop or train set and putter around. Or he'd go out to the yard and spend time there – anything it seemed but spend time with his family.

She also knew that what Russ did almost every night when he finished his four-to-twelve shift could not be considered lovemaking. Lovemaking included foreplay and loving actions – and there was none of that. It was pure lust and sex – done so he alone could release his own sexual tensions. It didn't seem to matter to him that Jenny was normally fast asleep when he got home from work. He just climbed aboard and had sex with her.

At first Jenny would lie awake after he'd finished rutting, not realising why she couldn't sleep. After reading books on the topic she realised that she was sexually frustrated. Russ would start to wake her up sexually, ejaculate then turn over, leaving her turned on, with no sexual release. Sex with Russ took as long as it took her to clean her teeth, but he gave nothing to her in return. Slowly but surely, she developed a mental switch that she used to keep herself from becoming aroused.

How annoyed and frustrated she felt when Russ accused her of being frigid. After that cruel comment they had another long-drawn out argument about how uncaring he was. Nothing changed.

Jenny was often puzzled by Russ's behaviour and wondered why he wouldn't discuss his feelings with her. She tried many times to talk to him about what he was feeling and concluded that he simply didn't trust her with that level of openness. This kept Russ and Jenny apart because of his inability to be intimate with her. Jenny concluded that it was likely caused by his upbringing by his Italian father who taught him to keep emotionally detached and separate and to suppress his softer emotions.

When he was upset, Russ often responded as if he was angry. He seemed able to show happiness and anger, but not feelings between those two emotions. When he felt anxious, disappointed, jealous, sad, hurt, rejected, stupid, intimidated, insecure, ashamed or ignored, his outward appearance showed only anger.

One time when Russ came storming home from work in a rage and woke the entire family, Jenny said, 'I can see you're distressed about something and understand that you don't want to talk to me about it now, but I can't stand by and condone your destructive behaviour. We have to talk about this because of the spin-off problems it's causing, not only for me, but for our children.'

He got her message, but still refused to talk about what had caused his rage.

Russ would often make lewd advances to Jenny in the presence of their children - running his hands over her breasts or surprising her when she was cooking by coming up behind her and putting his hands around her to grab her by the crotch. He knew this annoyed her but became angry when she shunned his advances. He didn't seem to understand that he repelled her rather than turned her on with these actions.

Russ had bad body odour and breath. Although he worked at a labouring job, he would only have one or two baths per week. He insisted on having baths instead of showers, because he expected Jenny to stop whatever she was doing to scrub his back. Instead of complying with his request, she sent one of the boys to do this chore. Russ seemed to believe this action would turn her on sexually, but it simply turned her off. He neglected his teeth and didn't clean them regularly, so he had bad breath. Even kissing him was distasteful. Besides - he smelled.

Being an efficient housekeeper, her household chores were often completed by noon, and she had the rest of the afternoon to put in time. She approached Russ about returning to work, but he made it abundantly clear that if she decided to go back to work, she'd still have to do all the work she normally did in their home. She attempted to work part-time for a while, but with small children to care for and all the work that had to be done around the home she gave up on the idea. Instead, she offered dressmaking out of her home and although it gave her exposure to others, she found that it didn't make enough money to warrant the time she spent on it.

To keep herself occupied and stimulated, she started learning different kinds of crafts. Macramé was all the rage, so she learned all the knots, found the hardest pattern she could find, did it well, and soon became bored with it. When she noticed that an old sofa set in her basement required recovering, she tackled the job head-on. After carefully removing the original covering, she made it into a pattern, and did an excellent job of re-upholstering the sofa. Her next project was refinishing their wooden dining room table. This involved seven weeks of hand-sanding the dowelled legs of the chairs and table then refinishing it with two coats of clear acrylic paint. Again, she was bored and looked around for anything else that would keep her mind occupied.

Jenny loved to read and became a voracious reader. However, she soon learned that Russ hated seeing her doing so when he was around. He seldom read anything and thought she was wasting her time when she did. When he spied her reading, he would ask her to put down her book and sit beside him on the sofa while he watched his sports programs. She wasn't into sports, so this was torture for her. She often left the living room and did ironing or some other chore, so she wouldn't have to waste her time watching sports. Jenny finally defied his wishes and read even though she knew it annoyed him.

Russ didn't seem to have empathy towards others. She recalled how Russ had failed to react when another man abused his wife in their presence. On one of their few evenings out, they'd gone to Russ's favourite tavern. That night, they met up with Russ's friend Grant Davidson who was there without his wife. 'Where's Betty?' Jenny asked.

'She's at home with the kids.' They had three children and were expecting a fourth even though Betty was just twenty-three. That evening Grant became so drunk, that Russ grabbed the keys out of his hand and drove him home while Jenny followed in their car. When they arrived, Russ helped Grant to his front door and beckoned to Jenny when Grant insisted that they come in for a cup of coffee. Grant gestured for them to sit at the kitchen table then staggered into the bedroom.

They heard him as he nudged Betty, 'Come on. Get up and make us some coffee.'

'Grant. Don't wake her up. We're going now.' Jenny said as she stood at the kitchen door.

'Oh no. She's getting up and will make us coffee.' Grant roared. Jenny took Russ's arm and tried to get him to leave. He gave her a dirty look and shook off her arm.

It was obvious that Betty had been deeply asleep and resisted having to get up. 'Put this on.' he said roughly as he handed her a housecoat.

Grant had Betty by the arm and pulled her roughly down the hallway then shoved her against the doorway into the kitchen. Betty was five months pregnant and winced when he again roughly shoved her against the kitchen wall.

'Make us some coffee.' he demanded.

Jenny looked at Russ to see what he was going to do about this violent behaviour; but he did nothing. She stepped in front of Betty and facing Grant said 'Grant, leave her alone. She's tired and Russ and I are leaving.'

Grant turned and stumbled into the bedroom. Jenny looked at Betty and asked, 'Are you going to be okay?'

Betty nodded, 'He'll be asleep in about five minutes.'

'Okay. We're going, as long as you think you'll be okay.' she added.

Betty nodded again and gave Jenny a quick hug as she left.

When Russ and Jenny got to their car Russ asked, 'Why did you do that?'

'Didn't you see him shove her against the wall?' she asked angrily.

'Yeah. But that's none of our business.' he stated.

'Don't you realise that she's five months pregnant and that shoving her like that could harm the baby? That's wife and child abuse!'

Russ just grunted and continued driving them home. It was several days before they had a normal conversation and even longer before Jenny spoke civilly to Grant. She phoned Betty the next morning to be sure she was all right and was assured that she was fine, and Betty thanked Jenny for her intervention.

A neighbour Barry Fellows, who was twice Jenny's age, sometimes came to the tavern with them. Barry was forever making sexual advances towards Jenny; sitting beside her and running his hand up and down her thigh. Jenny kept moving away from him to another seat, but he eventually would find some way to sit beside her again. Russ was aware of this, but just smiled and did nothing. It was almost as if he was proud of the way Jenny turned on this older man.

When Jenny was in her back yard playing with the children, she often caught Barry spying on her from his upstairs window two doors away. The most disturbing situation relating to Barry's actions came one night after they'd been at the tavern. Jenny just wanted to get home and go to bed but Russ went to Barry's place to drink more beer. About an hour later, Russ staggered home and woke Jenny saying that Barry had offered him a hundred dollars to spend the night with her. He seemed to be pleased at the man's comments - instead of defending her against such lewd suggestions. From then on, Jenny refused to go out if Barry was going to go with them. Several times Russ went alone when she refused to do so.

Chapter 26

When they'd been married for ten years, Russ announced, 'I've bought a part-ownership in a security police firm that uses German Shepherd and Doberman guard dogs to patrol warehouses and are used for riot control.'

'Why didn't you discuss this with me before you invested our money in this? We still owe Dad fifteen hundred dollars for the cottage supplies.'

He ignored her last statement and said, 'Well, I've been talking to Blair Hutchinson about this for several months and I finally decided to do it.'

'That still doesn't explain why you didn't discuss this with me before you made that decision!' she replied angrily.

'It's my money from Mom and Dad's home and the time I'm investing – it has nothing to do with you. The only thing that will affect you is that we will be keeping one of the guard dogs in a kennel I'm going to build in the back yard.'

'What if it bites the children?' she asked with concern.

'He's well trained and is gentle with children. His name is Thor and he's a well-trained German Shepherd guard dog. I've met him and seen him with Blair's children. He's very gentle with them. I'll be bringing him home as soon as I finish building his kennel.'

'What about your job with the railway?' Jenny asked.

'Oh, I'll still do that, but will do a bit of patrol work myself during my off hours.'

'So, you'll be spending even less time with me and the children!' she spat at him. Jenny knew the subject was closed when he abruptly walked out of the kitchen.

That Saturday, Russ had finished building the kennel and left to bring the dog home. The boys were very excited and couldn't wait to meet their new dog. When Russ arrived with Thor, Jenny realised that he was a very big dog and again felt apprehensive that he might be dangerous around the children. Russ introduced the dog to the boys – telling them to hold out their hands with the back of their hands towards the dog so Thor could know their scent. Mark walked up to the huge dog and very hesitantly held out his hand. Thor sniffed it – then his big tongue came out and he licked his hand. Mark smiled and patted the dog. Then it was Bruce's turn. He had no fear of this big dog and copied his older brother's actions. Soon the dog and the children were playing 'fetch the stick' in their back yard.

Then it was time for Thor to be introduced to baby Debbie. Jenny watched apprehensively as Russ led Thor into the house towards Debbie. Thor's tail began to wag as soon as he spotted the baby. He sniffed the baby and Jenny was positive she saw Thor grinning. He lay down quietly on the carpet beside her and Debbie gazed at him with her big brown eyes.

'I told you he was gentle,' reminded Russ.

'Yes, he does seem to have a nice temperament – doesn't seem at all to be a trained guard dog.'

'We have special words and signals we use when he's on duty, and he knows that if I or someone else is in uniform – he's on duty.' he explained.

Thor just loved Debbie and would sit patiently while she pulled herself up by hanging onto his fur. She even climbed on his back and lay upon him mumbling baby talk to him. When Russ held Debbie on his back, Thor patiently walked slowly across the living room. Debbie would laugh and ask for more.

However, they learned that they did have to be careful when other children came over. If they were rough-housing and got too boisterous, Thor became very protective of the boys. So, Thor had to be put in his kennel when other children came to play in their home or in their back yard.

Some evenings, other security police officers came to pick Thor up, so they could leave him in a warehouse overnight. Then they would return him to his kennel early in the morning. The officers wore smart uniforms and hats that slightly resembled police force uniforms but had the company logo on the armbands and front pockets. Most of these security officers were quite young, and lonely – especially Ron Baker whose family lived in a rural town far from where he had found work. Russ was usually at work when the officers came to collect Thor for guard duty and Jenny enjoyed their company. She often offered them a cup of coffee before they took Thor on duty. There was never anything sexual in these relationships – just two lonely people enjoying the companionship of another kind human being. Jenny found that she looked forward to those occasional coffee discussions.

Local newspapers once wrote an article about Thor's bravery. One of the city's A & W drive-in restaurants was having problems with rival gangs who chose their property as the venue for their battles. Soon customers refused to go near the restaurant. Because the regular police department couldn't afford to have an officer there all the time, A & W decided to hire one of Blair's patrol officers and guard dog to deal with the problem. Thor was the dog chosen to do so. His handler for that assignment, Neil Roberts, had not worked with him very often so did not know Thor's capabilities.

One evening it was obvious that the gangs were gathering, and Neil watched apprehensively as the gangs started towards each other across the parking lot. While the manager of the A & W called the police, Neil walked with Thor between the two gangs. At that point they were about forty feet away from each other. They carried chains, bars and knives so Neil was naturally apprehensive about what would happen with him in the middle of the gangs. He was not armed with a weapon except for the guard dog.

'Stop.' he shouted.

One gang paused in their advance, but the other group kept moving forward.

'Stop or I'll be forced to let the dog go.' Neil said as he felt Thor straining at his leash.

The second gang just laughed and kept moving closer to Neil and Thor. When they were about ten feet away Neil gave them a final warning. 'This is your last warning!'

The gang members looked at each other, nodded and kept advancing. Neil released the catch on the leash and gave Thor the order to attack. Later he admitted that he'd never seen anything so spectacular in his life. Thor crashed into the closest gang member, his fangs dug deep into the wrist holding the pipe. Then as quick as lightening he attacked the next man who wielded a chain. He tore the leather covered elbow of the arm holding the chain – ripping and shaking his elbow until the man dropped the chain. The next fellow turned around to run, but Thor tore a chunk of flesh off his buttock.

Neil yelled at the rest of the fleeing men to lie down. They promptly flung themselves face down on the road. One of them yelled, 'Call him off – we give up!'

Neil ordered Thor to stop and called him to his side – as he checked the gang on the other side of him. They too were face down on the concrete. Minutes later, two squad cars arrived, and the gangs were rounded up and taken into custody and the three injured gang members were taken to hospital. The local newspapers had sent a photographer to the site and they took a picture of Neil and Thor as Neil talked to the police officers about the attack.

The next week Thor was on duty at the Greyhound Bus Depot and having that article pinned to the wall was enough to stop any problems they had if Thor was patrolling there with a security police officer.

Not all Thor's assignments were as exciting. Often, he just spent a lonely night patrolling a warehouse or outdoor fenced compound of equipment or vehicles. There was one memorable occasion, however, when Thor was left in a warehouse. When Ron Baker picked him up in the morning, he found Thor standing guard beside a man who was lying face down on the floor of the warehouse. Any move the man made, caused Thor to growl at him

'I've been here since one o'clock last night. Damned dog wouldn't even let me up to go to the bathroom.' the hostage complained. Ron noted that his pants were wet.

Ron left Thor guarding the prisoner while he called the police and the owner. The police charged the man with break and enter and took him into custody. When the grateful owner arrived, Thor was rewarded with a nice juicy piece of steak.

Chapter 27

However even with the excitement of Thor's adventures and having the security officers visit, Jenny was still lonely and felt as if she was just putting in time. Her house was spotless, her children were happy, but a void was always there. She began asking herself, *"Is this all there is? If it is, I don't want it. I want a husband that I can communicate with, who will do more for his family than bring in his paycheque."*

Jenny tried to talk to Russ about it, but he scoffed at her. 'I just wish I had it as easy a life as you have.' was all he said.

One evening, Russ said that Blair Hutchinson, the owner of the security police firm wanted to talk to her. When he arrived, he explained to Jenny, 'As you know, we use guard dogs to patrol warehouses and they receive extensive training on what they're to do if they need to disarm a suspect. However, we've noticed a snag in the training of some of the younger guard dogs. They won't attack a woman even if she has a weapon. We're wondering if you could help out with that training.'

Jenny was surprised that he would ask her to do such a dangerous thing. She glanced at Russ and he smiled at her.

'I don't think that's a good thing for me to consider.' she replied. 'Suppose the dog bit me or hurt me badly? I can't chance that with children to care for.'

'You would wear protective gear. The dogs are trained to go for the weapon, not the throat or anywhere else in your body. The hand that held the weapon would be completely protected by thick padding.'

'Russ, what do you think about this?' she asked.

'I think you should do it. We also need women security workers too, so we would put you through the self-defence training courses.'

Jenny began to be interested in the idea. In the past Russ had balked at her working at all and it appeared that he would be solidly behind her if she decided to take the training to be a security police officer. It would finally allow her to do something stimulating for a change.

'I'll do what you want. When do you want me to start working with the dogs?' she asked.

'I'm so pleased,' said Blair. 'We can start tomorrow. I will pick you up and take you to the dog training area and try on the protective gear. We may have to adapt it somewhat because you're smaller than the male officers.'

So, the next day, with her heart thumping in fear, Jenny donned the protective gear and held a piece of pipe in her hand. She winced as the first almost full-grown dog came rushing at her, straining at the leash held by its dog handler. The dog growled and sank his fangs into the padding and wrenched the pipe out of her hand. The trainer called him off and praised him for doing such a good job and walked away. Soon he returned with another dog and gave it the command to attack. It looked around in confusion then walked up to Jenny and wagged his tail. His handler had to give him, the command to attack again and the dog finally realised that he was to attack the woman. He grabbed and shook the arm until Jenny released the pipe. They repeated this process until all six young dogs had removed the pipe from Jenny's hand.

The next week Jenny began self-defence training with three other women. It was a combination of Karate, Tae Kwon Do and Judo. They practiced the throws and defensive moves until they felt comfortable using them. Then came the test day when they faced men who were told to fight them hard. Jenny's attacker was several inches taller than she, but she gave him a hip toss that sent him plummeting to the carpet. He sat with a surprised look on his face. She saw Russ staring in amazement. She was astonished when he stepped forward to become her attacker. After having a moment of panic knowing how big and strong he was she assumed a defensive stance. He circled around and approached her from behind. Jenny swerved the opposite way than he expected and was able to use her body as a lever to flip him onto his back as well. Russ never forgave her for that.

Jenny felt unusual as she tried on her first security police uniform. It had been custom made because hers was the first female uniform they had ordered. She wore her hair in a French roll at the back of her head and placed the smart hat on top of it. 'Not bad.' she said as she saw how good she looked in the uniform.

Her first assignment as a security police officer was at a dance hall in downtown Winnipeg. There had been quite a few fights there and Blair's officers had been able to handle the troublemakers successfully. However, some of the troublemakers were women who started fights in the women's washrooms, so they needed female officers to handle such incidents.

That night, Jenny watched as two men started fighting. Her male co-worker stepped between them and stopped the fight. He'd just stepped back when Jenny spotted a third man behind the officer. He held a chair over his head and it was obvious that he was going to hit the officer with it. Jenny rushed to stand behind the attacker, bent her knees behind the man's knees that caused his legs to collapse beneath him. She quickly stepped back as the man and the chair clattered to the floor. Jenny stepped forward again and quickly cuffed him. Her co-worker turned in surprise to see what had happened. The management called the police and the three troublemakers were arrested for assault and causing a disturbance.

Then Jenny worked as a 'professional shopper.' Professional shoppers are used by all major department stores to ensure that the clerks are acting honestly. They suspected a clerk of working a scam and Jenny was asked to help catch her. Jenny purchased an item, handed the suspected clerk the exact change, popped the item into her shopping bag and rushed off saying she couldn't wait for the sales slip. Another security person watched to see whether the clerk rang up the sale or pocketed the money. She pocketed the money, was arrested and taken to jail. That day they caught a ring of clerks that had been operating out of one of their major department stores.

A few months later, Blair had a call from a very influential man in their city. There was a special evening planned, and those coming to it were encouraged to arrive at the function in unusual ways. Some had hired horses to pull sleighs, some came on horseback, others drove old cars, and another came in a skidoo. This man called Blair to see if he could arrange for him and his wife to arrive by dog sled. Blair phoned around and was able to arrange for a dog team to be brought down from Churchill, Manitoba for the affair.

Several days before the couple's special evening, the dogs, sled and their driver arrived at Blair's kennel. Most teams of sled dogs consist of anywhere from three to two dozen dogs. This team consisted of seven lovely animals, mainly Siberian Huskies and Alaskan Malamute dogs, but the leader of the pack or 'king' dog was a cross between an Alaskan Husky and a timber-wolf. These sled dogs were accustomed to running anywhere from five to eighty miles or more per day at an average speed of twenty miles per hour. All but the lead dog were hitched in tandem, with harnessed pairs of dogs pulling on tug lines attached to a central gang-line. Their driver exercised the dogs every day and offered rides to the families of the security officers. So, Jenny and her children were bundled up, placed in the sled and had the thrill of riding behind the lovely animals.

On the special night the man and his wife made front page headlines in the local newspaper as they arrived at the affair in the dog sled. Everyone was disappointed when the dog team left and returned to Churchill in the far North.

But things were no better between Russ and Jenny. At home, she still spent most of her time alone with the children and knew she could no longer tolerate Russ's nonparticipation in both her and their children's lives. One Friday night after Russ had literally ignored Jenny and the children during his days off, she sat thinking about how sad her life had become. She couldn't remember the last time she'd laughed when Russ was around and acknowledged that she didn't even laugh when she watched funny television shows any more. The only time she remembered laughing was when she watched the antics of her children. Yes, she'd certainly lost her sense of humour and she wanted it back!

So, what was she going to do? 'I've had enough of living this half-life,' she decided, 'and I'm going to do something about it!'

When she phoned her brother Jeff and his wife Marion to ask if she and the children could stay with them for a few days, Jeff replied 'It will be an awfully tight fit, but sure come on over!' She hoped that Russ would finally understand that she was serious and take some steps to improve their family situation.

After two days, as Jenny had hoped, Russ came to beg her to return home with the children. 'Please come home. I miss you and the kids.' he said as he sat on the sofa at Jeff's home.

'Russ, I'm serious this time. Unless things change drastically, I don't want to live with you any more.' she said emphatically.

'What do you want me to do?' he asked sheepishly.

'I want us to go to a marriage counsellor and see whether we can turn things around.' she said insistently.

'Why do we have to bring in an outsider? Can't we settle this between us?' he questioned.

'No, I've tried for years to get you to listen to me but time after time you've ignored me completely. I refuse to let that happen this time. Now will you agree to see a marriage counsellor?'

'All right. But please come home now.' he pleaded.

The next day Jenny made an appointment with a marriage counsellor. When they arrived at his office, the counsellor talked to them together, then separately. Then he asked them both back into his office to ask more questions and give his recommendations.

'Russ, are you happy with how Jenny is managing your home and the children?'

'Oh yes, she does a great job.'

'Why do you think she's unhappy?'

'I think it's because I spend so much time working and don't spend enough time with her and the children.'

'How about your social life? Do you do things together that you both like?'

'We go to the tavern about every two weeks.'

'Does Jenny like going to the tavern on your nights out?'

'No, not really. I guess she doesn't.'

'Do you ever go where she wants to go?'

'She always wants us to go to a restaurant or a dinner theatre. That costs too much money, so we don't go there.'

'Do you think that's fair to Jenny if you never go where she wants to go?'

'I guess not.'

'When's the last time the two of you were away from the children to enjoy a weekend together.' he said as he glanced from Russ to Jenny.

'We've never been away from the kids for more than an evening out since Mark was born.' replied Jenny.

'Well, I think it's time you planned on a 'wicked weekend' so you can get the spark back into your life. And Russ, I also think that you should change working your four-to-twelve shift and have normal weekends. You mentioned that your company was willing to have you do this. Why have you continued with the shift-work now that you have a wife and children that want and need you home in the evenings and weekends?'

'I like working that shift.' Russ said stiffly. 'I hate driving in rush hour traffic and that's what I'd face coming and going to work if I worked the day shift. With this shift, I travel before the rush hour and there's hardly any traffic when I drive home after midnight.'

'Well, will you at least think about what it would mean to your family if you were at home with them more?'

'Okay, I'll think about it.' Russ reluctantly agreed.

'So, when do you think the two of you can get away for that 'wicked weekend?' he asked.

'First we will have to decide where we will go. Then I'll have to see if I can find someone to look after the children for the days we're away.' Jenny replied.

When they returned home, Jenny and Russ discussed where they would go for their 'wicked weekend.' Russ wanted to go to their cottage at the lake, but Jenny felt they could go there anytime. She wanted to go somewhere special – some place that was more romantic. They finally agreed they would drive to Thunder Bay and stay in a motel that had a swimming pool for a few days. Because Ian and Martha were now living in Victoria, she spoke to her mother's friend Evelyn Jenkins who offered to come over and care for the children while they were away.

Jenny looked forward to leaving the next Wednesday morning. They would have all day Wednesday, Thursday and part of Friday to enjoy each other's company until Russ had to return to work on Friday at four o'clock. Jenny was more than a bit upset that he still hadn't spoken with his boss about changing his work schedule, so she hoped she'd be able to discuss that further with him during their short holiday.

The Sunday before they were to leave, Russ had just finished his breakfast and was having a cup of coffee when he said, 'The boss told me last night that I have to work on Wednesday and Thursday evenings. So, we can't go away this week.'

Jenny looked incredulously at him and thought, *You're the one who decided to work those extra nights – not your boss.*

Instead, she said, 'How could you do this Russ? Our marriage is at stake here! Don't you realise how important it is for us to get away.'

Russ just shrugged his shoulders and said, 'We'll go away another time.'

'When? Give me a date!' she almost shouted at him.

'Quit pushing me!' he bellowed as he got up from the table so abruptly that his chair crashed to the floor. 'I don't want to hear about this again!'

Jenny realised that he was not going to change. She knew he had not tried to change his shifts, so he was completely ignoring the advice of the family counsellor. He would not change – that was obvious. So, was she willing to stay with him? She began seriously thinking that the only solution would be for them to separate for good.

Chapter 28

Shortly after speaking with the counsellor, when they'd been married eleven years, Jenny became ill. The children had been home with the flu, but her illness seemed to go on far too long. She wondered if she had the flu or if her illness was due to the tension and stress she lived under, so decided to see Dr. Sims. She sat lethargically in his office. After his examination, Dr. Sims smiled as he dropped the bombshell, 'Congratulations, you're pregnant.'

'This can't be happening!' she said. It was the last thing she'd anticipated. She'd faithfully taken birth control pills since her last pregnancy, so she and Russ believed they were safe from pregnancy the few times they'd had sex lately.

'I can't go through this again!' she groaned.

Dr Sims pointed out that she did have options, 'You realise, that with your gestation history, you have the option of terminating your pregnancy. Should you choose to continue your pregnancy, it will be imperative that you obtain help at home and become almost bedridden during your third trimester.'

For the first time in her life, she contemplated the distasteful idea of having an abortion. Memories of her past two lost pregnancies crowded her mind.

And now that she felt her family was complete – to be told she was pregnant again – well things were different this time. Losing two almost full-term babies was bad enough – but trying again – that was another thing to consider. The possibility was high that she would deliver another premature baby, so she'd have to consider carefully the option of continuing her pregnancy. Jenny loved children, and her feelings about ending a life were very strong, but what was best for her family?

A new baby had been started. Like every newly pregnant woman she felt the excitement of having started a new life. What would it be – a boy or a girl? Would it be healthy – have all its fingers and toes? Or would she go into early labour again and be tossed into the tornado of feelings involved with losing another baby. Would she suffer the heart-wrenching emptiness she remembered from the other two times her babies had died? Could she withstand the long period of time it would take her to start to function normally again? Would she suffer from weeks of depression as she had those other times? Would it be worth taking the chance again of having to live through such a nightmare? Or would the baby be fine this time?

Then she remembered her other pregnancies when the first flutter of the butterfly in her lower abdomen announced to her that a new life was making itself felt. She remembered touching her abdomen just over the fluttering feeling, her face full of wonderment. Later on in her pregnancies she recalled feeling the thumps from an arm or leg stretch of the developing baby. And in Mark's case the battering she'd had to her rib cage given by her big beautiful boy?

Could she cut off the life of a baby just because she and Russ had been careless? Didn't this child deserve a chance to live like any other baby? It wasn't as if they couldn't afford another baby – oh sometimes the budget was strained, but they could afford this baby. So what was she going to tell the doctor? Or should she abort the baby and follow through with leaving Russ? What a decision to have to make!

She knew she'd have to consult Russ about it even though she and Russ hadn't been getting along very well since he'd ignored the marriage counsellor's advice. That's why they hadn't had sex very often. Their most recent battle still revolved around the hours he worked. He still refused to accept the day shift with weekends off offer that was open to him and didn't seem to understand why she was so angry with him. 'I bring in the paycheque – what more do you want from me?' he asked.

Jenny knew that until that issue was settled, the cold war would continue. And yet when she had gone to Jeff's for those few days, he had told her how much he missed her and the children. It didn't make sense to her.

Did he or did he not love her?

She brought her mind back to her current situation – finding herself pregnant again. She'd have to find the right moment to speak to him. Several times she prepared herself to tell him she was pregnant, so they could discuss their options, but couldn't find the right moment to do so. Time passed, and soon it was too late to safely end her pregnancy. In hindsight she realised that she would never have seriously considered aborting her baby.

In the interim, she'd received a letter from her parents inviting her family to visit them in Victoria as soon as school was out for the summer. Ian and Martha had retired and when Jenny was fully recovered from her car accident, they'd moved to Victoria, on Vancouver Island. Jenny decided to take them up on their offer, but because Russ said he couldn't get time off (Jenny believed he hadn't even asked) she and the children went alone.

After they arrived at her parent's home and Jenny phoned Russ, he was so cold and uncommunicative that she found it difficult to say anything to him about the pregnancy. She didn't tell her parents either.

Martha and Ian made the children's visit so much fun, that they and the children begged Jenny to let them stay longer. 'What's the sense of taking them home to such a hostile atmosphere?' she thought as she nodded her consent to the children.

Jordan, a neighbourhood boy came over quite often, and one day brought two ponies so the children could ride them. Jordan even sat on one and held Debbie in front of him so she could enjoy a ride as well. Because they had so much fun, Jordan brought the ponies over several other times.

Ian taught Mark how to golf, while Martha taught Bruce. Jenny laughed as she watched them swing the clubs.

It made her recall a time when she was about eleven and Ian offered to teach her how to golf. He'd taken her to the far end of the nearby school yard in Winnipeg to practice her golf swing. She remembered trundling along carrying a bucket full of old golf balls. Ian carried a driver for himself and a smaller borrowed one for Jenny.

'Watch how I do it then copy the way to stand and swing,' he explained.

Jenny tried to copy his stance, but Ian had to go behind her to show her the kind of grip her hands were to make on the club. She practiced the crossed hands grip and made an imaginary swing with the club.

'You have to watch what your feet are doing too.' he said as he demonstrated the proper way to place her feet and turn her legs.

'Now let's practice swinging the club a few times before we actually hit a ball.' he suggested.

Next, he inserted a golf tee into the hard soil of the school ground, placed the ball on it, took the proper stance, and hit the ball almost to the end of the school ground. He hit several more. Then it was Jenny's turn.

She made a few practice swings then copied his actions of placing a tee and putting a ball on the tee. Ian pointed to the spot she was to use as a guideline for where he wanted her to hit the ball. She took a mighty swing that connected solidly with the ball. The next sound they heard was the sound of breaking glass. Jenny had hit the ball so hard it had gone right through one of the school windows!

Ian looked incredulously at Jenny. She had hit the ball far farther than he had and straight for the mark he'd given her, but much further.

'Oops. I guess this wasn't a very good idea. I had no idea you would be so good, especially on your first swing. We'd better go to a driving range from now on.' Ian said sheepishly.

They left the school ground, but Jenny didn't know whether Ian informed the school authorities about who sent the golf ball through the school window.

Jenny had learned that she was not able to play golf after her car accident because doctors had advised that the swinging action would likely hurt her back.

She and the children's three-week holiday stretched into six weeks, so by the time Jenny returned to her home in Winnipeg, she was four and a half months pregnant and starting to show. It was hard to hide her condition and she wondered how she could break the news to Russ. Because of his hostile behaviour, telling him on the phone was out of the question. As soon as she got home, she gave him a baby card that congratulated prospective parents. On it she had written, 'Congratulations – You're going to be a Daddy!'

He gave a questioning look at her abdomen and asked, 'Why didn't you tell me earlier?'

'We certainly weren't getting along very well when I learned about the pregnancy, and I couldn't find an ideal time to tell you. Besides with my history there'll be less time friends and family will have to wonder whether I can carry the pregnancy to full term.'

They didn't discuss the situation further. Her pregnancy progressed normally, but Jenny remembered Dr. Sim's caution that she absolutely must obtain help during the last trimester of her pregnancy. Her baby was due in early January, so in September, she started discussing the need to obtain housekeeping and childcare help for her. When the time came to get help, Russ's answer was, 'We can't afford it. We'll just have to manage somehow. I'll do what I can, and the boys can help out more. There's no reason why they can't do the laundry and wash floors!'

This made sense, but who would run around after their two-year-old daughter Debbie, provide meals, do the shopping and the thousands of other duties when he was at work?

Jenny knew Russ wouldn't help much himself and rather than start another argument, decided to make the best of things. She tried to rest more but found it almost impossible with three children and one of them a toddler. Just keeping track of what two-year-old Debbie was doing was a monumental task. Jenny felt lucky that she was an easy child to care for, had a sweet disposition and was able to amuse herself for a much longer time than the boys had be able to do at her age. The boys did their best and helped as much as they could. Mark took over the laundry and helped care for Debbie. Bruce became very proficient at washing floors, doing dishes and generally cleaning up. They did an admirable job and she was amazed at how much help a nine- and seven-year-old could be.

Chapter 29

Her pregnancy continued to be uneventful and she began to hope things would be different this time. At least that is until the first morning of November when she had just entered her seventh month of pregnancy. Everything appeared normal when she got up that morning, but when she went to the bathroom she noticed that she was spotting lightly. Her heart raced, and she realised the signs. The thought, *"Here we go again! – I'm in trouble again."* entered her mind. Russ was home and she told him what had happened. She also phoned Dr. Sims, who told her she must have full bed rest from then on.

Russ looked after the children, gave them lunch, put Debbie down for her afternoon nap then started packing his lunch box.

'What are you doing?' Jenny asked.

'Making my lunch for work.' he replied.

'Are you going to work?' Jenny asked incredulously.

'Yes, I am.' was his simple reply.

'And what about the bed rest I'm supposed to get?' Jenny was getting madder and madder.

'Just tell the boys what you need done. Or why don't you phone one of your friends to come and look after you?'

'It's up to you to make some arrangements. When are you going to start helping me for a change?' she said as she waited for his answer.

'You'll do fine. The boys have been doing a great job. By the way, I hope you haven't forgotten that I'm going hunting with a few of my co-workers after work tonight. I won't be back until tomorrow some time.'

Jenny simply couldn't believe Russ could be so thoughtless. At that moment she really hated him. She just glared at him and didn't speak a word to him before he left for work. That night the boys pitched in and were able to make sandwiches for dinner. Debbie climbed into bed with Jenny and they spent an enjoyable evening reading books. The boys also joined her, then Mark helped Debbie get ready for bed. Before Mark went to bed himself, he asked Jenny if she needed anything else. 'I'd love a cup of tea. You know how to make it don't you?'

'Sure Mom. I'll be right with you.' Mark replied.

He arrived shortly after with a steaming cup of tea with just a bit of milk and sugar the way she liked it. She gave him a hug and said, 'Thanks Mark for helping me out so much. Good night. See you in the morning.'

That night Russ did not come home after work, so she knew he'd gone hunting with his buddies as planned. Why they would go hunting at night she couldn't figure. It was hunting season but didn't think people could shoot at animals at night.

Late the next morning Russ came home – without his rifle. He and his buddies had been caught 'spotlighting' for deer with a powerful light and had bagged an adult male. The Royal Canadian Mounted Police had heard the shots and had caught them loading the deer into the back of their vehicle. All their rifles were confiscated for three months and later they paid hefty fines for the offence.

Jenny just listened while he told his tale. She was still furious with him and made it plain to him with her silence and dirty looks. She was still trying to stay in bed, but more and more it became obvious that the boys couldn't be expected to look after their two-year-old sister forever. They wanted to go outside to play, so Jenny sent them off and got up to sit on the living room sofa. Debbie played quietly with her toys but needed Jenny to get up once in a while to get her a drink, a tissue to wipe her nose and other necessities. Russ carried on as normal ignoring the danger he was putting Jenny in by not providing her with the care she desperately needed.

One week after she started spotting, her water broke. Jenny wasn't overly surprised and after she had cleaned herself up and changed her clothing she phoned Dr. Sims. He instructed her to go directly to the hospital stating, 'We'll have to try everything we can to discourage you from going into full labour.'

After she hung up she thought, 'How am I going to get there and who will look after the children?' Russ was on an errand, so she sent Mark next door to get help. Agnes Evans' daughter Denise agreed to look after the children while Agnes drove Jenny to the hospital.

Before getting into Agnes's car, Jenny placed a thick bath towel on the seat. On the way to the hospital, Jenny couldn't help thinking, *"Time, I need more time! This baby won't survive unless I can hold off delivery. If only I can hold on for another two or three weeks, we'll probably make it. Maybe if I'm in the hospital I can finally get the bed rest I'm supposed to have."*

When she arrived at the hospital she was soaked again from the amniotic fluid and was glad she'd remembered to take the large towel with her. Thankfully she had not felt any labour pains. When Dr. Sims examined her, he told her this was a good sign.

After she was settled in her room, her nurse attached a foetal monitor to her abdomen. Jenny's eyes widened when she heard the steady, but very fast, heartbeat of her unborn child and watched the screen showing the blip, blip, blip that showed proof of her child's healthy existence. After an hour, the nurse had to disconnect the machine for another woman who was having a difficult delivery.

Jenny wondered what was keeping Russ. He finally arrived at three o'clock explaining that Denise Evans from next door would continue looking after the children until he came home from work at midnight.

'You're going to work, knowing that I might lose another baby tonight?'

'Well, what do you expect me to do?' he asked quizzically.

'You could stay with me and at least pretend that you care what happens to me and our child!' she almost screamed at him.

They had another heated argument and by the time Russ stormed out of the hospital, Jenny realised that she was on her own - again. She also realised that she had a raging headache. Jenny couldn't remember when she'd last had a headache. It soon became unbearable, so she rang for the nurse and asked if she could have something to ease the pain. The nurse left to contact Dr. Sims.

While she was gone, everything seemed to go wrong for Jenny. Although there was another bed in her room, it wasn't occupied, so she didn't have anyone else to recognise her difficulties. She was holding her forehead, when she suddenly felt her first wrenching labour pain. This contraction was far stronger than those that normally accompanied the onset of labour. It was more like the kind of pain she would expect to have in the later stages of labour. In addition, Jenny realised that she felt icy cold, was perspiring heavily and began to shiver so violently that her shaking body moved the bed.

'This isn't right!' she moaned. 'This has never happened before! What's happening to me?' She searched for the bell and couldn't find it and wondered whether she was going to pass out before she could summon help.

Thankfully, a nurse appeared, took her temperature, and rushed out of the room. She returned with and applied several warm, flannelette sheets and a blanket that felt as if they had just come out of a dryer. How soothing they felt. Soon Jenny stopped shivering and recognised that her labour pains had stopped as well. By five o'clock she felt almost normal and wondered what had happened to her.

'We've called Dr. Sims to let him know about your fever, and that you had several strong labour pains. I've checked you and it appears that you haven't started dilating, so we may still be in luck and can hold off delivery for a while.'

While Jenny waited for Dr. Sims arrival, she tried to remain calm. It felt very soothing to lie under the warm blankets, and she was pleased to note that she had stopped perspiring and shivering. She felt so comfortable that she removed the top blanket, sat up and read a magazine for half an hour. While she read, she found herself running her hand over her swollen abdomen.

Her calmness ended when she recognised that something was dreadfully wrong. Her normally very active baby was suddenly very still. Then came the realisation that since her fever episode, she couldn't remember feeling the baby move. Her hand reached for the bell.

'I haven't felt my baby move since I had the fever and I'm really worried. Could you hook up that foetal monitor again, so I know the baby's okay?' she asked.

As the nurse checked her abdomen with a stethoscope, her frown confirmed that Jenny's concern was warranted. 'I'll see what's keeping your doctor.' she stated as she swiftly left the room.

Twenty minutes later, Dr. Sims arrived, listened to the baby's heartbeat, and declared. 'Your baby's in trouble. I don't think we have any recourse but to do an immediate caesarean. I'll see if I can find a specialist to do it.'

'Has the hospital contacted my husband since I started having trouble?' she asked.

'Yes, we have, and I thought he'd be here by now. I'll make the arrangements for the surgery to be done. In the meantime, I'll be starting you on antibiotics to fight the infection.' he added as he left the room.

Jenny knew her caesarean would have to be done right away, so became more and more frantic as time raced on. Two hours passed before Dr. Sims returned with the obstetrician Dr. Miller, who would do the surgery. Dr. Miller carefully listened to the baby's heartbeat, shook his head and said the simple distressing words, 'It's too late – the baby's dead.'

He patted Jenny's arm as he continued speaking to Dr. Sims, 'We might as well wait until she goes into labour naturally. Because she's had that 105° temperature earlier, the longer we can hold off delivery, the better. In the meantime, I want her to have something to help her sleep and keep her muscles relaxed. The longer we have to fight the infection before she goes into labour, the better it will be for her.'

He looked directly at Jenny and patted her again. 'I'm sorry this happened. I wish I'd been called earlier in your pregnancy – we may have been able to save your baby.'

'What caused the infection Doctor?' she asked quietly.

'When your water broke, it left you very vulnerable to infection.'

The doctors left the room, but Jenny could still hear what they said as they stood outside her closed door. 'She may not make it through the night unless her fever goes down. Let's hope and pray that she rallies and doesn't go back into labour until tomorrow or later.'

Their voices faded away as they walked down the hall, so Jenny couldn't hear more. The knowledge that her own life was in danger crowded her thoughts and she wondered whether she was going to die. Then her thoughts turned to the plight of her unborn child. 'You poor little waif,' she crooned as she ran her hand over her distended abdomen. 'You didn't stand a chance, did you? Maybe I'll be joining you soon.'

A nurse arrived with more antibiotics and something to help her sleep. Jenny wondered where Russ was and when he would arrive. The medication helped her drift off, but she awoke when Russ opened the door to her room. She felt the cold air coming from his jacket as he stood by her bed. She squinted at the clock and had to work to overcome her double vision. It was nine o'clock, five hours after he had first been told she was in trouble. 'What happened?' he asked.

She was still light-headed from the medication as she unemotionally told him about the baby being dead and the danger she would be in if she went into labour. He sat at her side silently but didn't offer any kind of sympathy or words of comfort. She noticed that he had not touched her since he came into the room nor uttered any words of sympathy about what she was going through. He finally suggested, 'Why don't you try to go back to sleep?'

"*So much for sympathy and support,*" she thought sadly as she drifted off again.

The clock showed it was just after midnight when she awoke again. The hospital was as quiet as a tomb. She was dreadfully thirsty and looked around to ask Russ to get her some water. He wasn't there, so she rang for the nurse. She asked for a glass of water and asked about her husband. 'He went home shortly after you went to sleep and said he'd be back in the morning.'

There's always a final straw that breaks a relationship. Thoughts raged through her mind, "*He left me here alone – knowing I might die during the night! How could he care so little about me, that he'd leave me to face this alone.*" She realised then, that Russ had never been there when she really needed him. During every crisis in their marriage, she'd had to face things alone.

That horrible night she made two stunning discoveries. The first was the confirmation that she'd have to deliver her dead baby alone - and secondly - that her marriage was over; this time for good. Thoughts of death permeated her thoughts and she was filled with sadness and despair. How could she survive this night alone? Who could she call to ask if they would come and stay with her? Calling any of her friends was out of the question because it was the middle of the night and she was so ashamed of Russ's desertion. She considered calling her mother but realised that by the time she would arrive from Victoria, the crisis would be over. How she craved having someone's sympathetic and supportive shoulder to cry on. How alone and empty she felt!

The nurse returned and hooked up more antibiotics to her intravenous line and gave her more medication to help her sleep. Jenny drifted off, but in what seemed like seconds, was rudely awakened by a labour pain so severe, that she cried out in pain.

When she realised that she was perspiring badly and shivering uncontrollably, she moaned, *"Oh God, here we go again."*

Her teeth chattered, and she rolled herself into a ball trying to minimise the pain. The contraction ended, and she searched for the bell. She found herself hesitating as thoughts swirled in her head. *"All I have to do, is let this happen. If I don't press this bell I can let myself die."*

As soon as this idea surfaced, the image of three little faces flashed before her eyes and she pushed the thoughts out of her mind. She knew that Russ would make a terrible single parent to their three children.

"No, I'm not going to let that happen. My children depend on me too much." She pushed the bell and within seconds, the nurse arrived stripped off her blankets and put another set of warmed ones on her. Again, as if a miracle had happened, she stopped shivering. Unfortunately, her labour pains didn't stop, and she gradually went through the stages of labour.

Between contractions, the medication made her feel as if she were detached from her body, but the wracking pains soon brought her back to reality. By five thirty that morning, she realised that she was beginning to feel an urge to bear down, so called the nurse. The nurse checked her, but said, 'You still have a while to go. I'll check you again in fifteen minutes.' she said as she left the room.

Ten minutes later Jenny delivered her dead baby - in her bed - in her hospital room – completely alone.

Chapter 30

She lay spent for a few moments then sat up and examined her dead baby. It had been another boy. She patted him gently, and with an eerie calmness, rang for the nurse. It was bedlam after that. The nurse was in tears and kept apologising for not being there when Jenny needed her. Dr. Sims arrived to help deliver the afterbirth and motioned for the nurse to leave the room with the baby.

Jenny and her bed were freshened, and a new antibiotic started. In a few minutes, her door opened and the nurse who'd been sobbing earlier, entered with a flannelette bundle and cautiously asked, 'Would you like to see your baby now that he's been cleaned up?'

Jenny extended her arms and tenderly unwrapped the layers of flannelette until the tiny naked body was fully exposed. She examined his little hands and feet and marvelled at the beautiful child her body had created.

'He certainly was perfect - wasn't he?' she stated. 'What a shame that circumstances beyond his and my control snuffed out his little life.'

She carefully re-wrapped the body and handed him back to the nurse who left the room. Jenny had never felt so alone in her life. She cried for hours and finally drained herself of tears.

It was three o'clock that afternoon before Russ arrived and he wasn't alone. Martha's plane had just arrived from Victoria half an hour before. Jenny brushed Russ away and reached for the solace of her mother's arms.

'I was so alone, Mom – I wish you could have been here to hold me and help me through this.' Martha held her daughter and they cried together. As Martha straightened up Jenny sent a scathing look in Russ's direction. She'd never forgive Russ for his desertion of her that night.

'I'll stay with you as long as you need me.' her mother promised. She was staying with her son Jeff and his family because there was no place for her to sleep at Jenny's home now that Debbie had the spare room.

Dr. Sims kept Jenny in the hospital for another twenty-four hours to fight the infection, but early the next day, he agreed to discharge her. Jenny's arms and mind felt so empty – again no baby to take home.

She wondered how she could go on being a mother to her children knowing that she hated their father and didn't want to live with him. Because it was his day off, she called Russ to pick her up.

'Okay, I'll be there in about half an hour.' he replied.

Jenny went to the closet in her room to change into her clothing and realised that she didn't have any clean clothes – just the soiled ones she'd been admitted in. She hadn't reminded Russ to bring fresh ones, but surely, he would know that she couldn't come home wearing the garments she wore when she arrived at the hospital? They had been put into a plastic bag and were still wet from when her water broke.

She sighed and sat in her housecoat waiting for Russ to come. When he arrived, she asked him for her change of clothing. He shrugged his shoulders and said, 'You didn't ask for any.'

'Did you really expect me to come home in these?' she asked as she threw the plastic bag of wet clothing at him. She decided that her only choice was to wear her bras, the top she had been wearing when she was admitted and her housecoat.

When they arrived at their home her spirits rose when Martha and her children greeted her with hugs. She reminded herself why she had decided to live instead of giving in to the overwhelming grief she'd felt when she knew that Russ had deserted her. It was hard for her to retain any semblance of normal life after her traumatic experience, but she knew she had to do so for her self-preservation and for her children.

Chapter 31

After Jenny returned home from the hospital, she and Martha had many long talks. Jenny withheld nothing from her. They talked for hours.

'You know you're welcome to come to Victoria. We can find a rental place for you and the kids that's near our place.'

'Mom I've been through such turmoil, I think I want to wait a few months to regain my health and emotional well-being before I take the drastic step of leaving Russ. I'm in no condition physically, emotionally or mentally to fight him if he asked for custody of the children.'

'I can only stay with you another week – I have to get back to your father. Is there anyone else who can help you through this emotional minefield?'

'I guess I could go back to the family counsellor, but that costs money and I'm going to have to start saving my pennies for when we leave.'

'How about Reverend Thompson? He's the one who married you and buried your babies. Possibly he can help you deal with the break-up as well.'

Jenny had always respected Reverend Thompson. He was a kind, compassionate man who must have had several psychology degrees, because he was so good at understanding people's problems. He had conducted the funerals for her babies and had officiated at Nellie's funeral. 'Yes, maybe that's what I should do. I'll talk to him.'

Jenny phoned and made an appointment. He was able to see her the next day. Martha was relieved that Jenny would have another support person to replace her when she returned to Victoria.

Reverend Thompson greeted Jenny warmly, 'I'm so sorry you lost another baby. You must be devastated.' Because the baby was stillborn, they did not have a funeral for the infant.

'Yes I am, but I didn't just lose a baby this time. My marriage is over as well.' she announced.

Jenny told him everything that had happened, not only about the most recent problems with Russ but how lonely and sad she'd been through most of her marriage. She made it clear that the only thing she thought Russ had contributed to their marriage was his sperm and his paycheque. It was two hours later when she finally finished revealing everything to him.

'I'm sorry Reverend, I'm probably keeping you from doing other more important things.' she said as she realised how long they had been talking.

'Right now – you are the most important thing! Now, what are your plans for the future?' he enquired.

'I plan on leaving Russ, but realise that I'm far too fragile emotionally, mentally and physically at the moment to go through the trauma of another crisis. I think I need several months to get my strength back and get emotionally back on track. Right now, I'm a wreck.'

'I have to agree with your plans. I advise people not to waste their time on others who won't support them in their time of need. It appears that many times Russ has not supported you during your time of need.' he added, then continued, 'How do you think you can regain your strength?'

'I plan on doing things *I* want to do for a change. I need to get out more – to get more involved in doing things for *me* instead of for everybody else. I think that's the most important thing I need to do, to get feeling better about myself.'

'I agree wholeheartedly. How do you intend to do that?' he enquired.

Jenny thought for a moment. 'I've always loved swimming – I want to get back into that. Possibly get a teaching licence and teach swimming.'

'Sounds like a good plan to me.' he said as he nodded his head.

'I'll play it by ear for a while and fit in other things as I think of them.'

'Would you like to continue having talks with me – possibly once a week – even if it's just on the telephone?' he enquired.

'That would be great. I don't have anyone else I can talk to – my parents live in Victoria and they're getting on in years. They've been very supportive, but I hate to keep bothering them all the time. They feel too helpless living so far away.'

'Okay, that sounds good to me.' he agreed, 'now, do you feel a bit better about your future?'

'Yes. You've been wonderful – I feel as if a huge load has been taken off my shoulders. I really want to do what is best for all of us – not just me.'

'Shall we set up an appointment for next week – say the same day and the same time?' he asked.

'That will be fine. And thank you so much for being there for me.' she said gratefully.

As Jenny drove home from the church, she felt so much better. When she got home Martha immediately recognised the difference in her demeanour by observing the spring in her step and the gleam in her eye. She'd really been worried about Jenny. She'd never seen her as far down and beaten as she appeared since losing her last baby.

Jenny told her mother about what had transpired at her meeting with Reverend Thompson. Martha felt content that it was safe to return to Victoria knowing that Jenny's welfare would be well taken care of by the kindly Reverend Thompson.

Three weeks after Jenny's baby was born and Martha had gone home, Antonio's wife Jean gave birth to their first child—a little girl they named Kathryn. Jenny knew she should go over to see the new baby but kept putting it off. She realised that she was jealous of Jean, that she had a live baby.

"This is foolishness." she said to herself one morning. *"I'm going over to see that baby."*

177

It was one of the hardest things Jenny had ever forced herself to do. The boys were in school, but she took Debbie with her.

When Jenny saw the baby, she just stared at her in shock. Kathryn was wearing the little sweater, bonnet and bootie outfit she'd knit for her own baby. Jenny's face was as white as a sheet and Jean recognised that she should not have put on that outfit—especially since Jenny was still raw from losing her baby.

'How did you get that outfit?' whispered Jenny.

'Russ brought it and a box of baby things last week. Didn't he tell you he was giving them to me?' Jean asked.

Jenny simply answered, 'No.'

"How could Russ have done this to me? Jenny wondered. What kind of monster would torture his wife this way?"

Now she hated Russ even more. Jean made a cup of coffee while Kathryn slept in her little cot. Jenny, who normally would have asked to hold the baby, found she was repelled by the idea.

On her way home, she phoned Reverend Thompson to see if he had time to see her that afternoon. He was available and had his secretary stayed with Debbie while he talked to Jenny.

Jenny poured her heart out to him, sobbing with great wracking waves of sorrow. She'd just begun to feel better but had been thrown back into her pit of despair by Russ's latest callous act.

Reverend Thompson soothed her and reminded her about the things she had decided to do to boost herself mentally and emotionally. She wiped her face and took some deep breaths.

I'd like to teach you some relaxation techniques you can use whenever you feel the pressure building up.' he suggested.

He walked her through the process and by the time Jenny left his office, she felt rejuvenated and vowed not to let Russ ruin her life for much longer.

Chapter 32

When Jenny enquired about training as a swimming instructor, she learned that before she could become one, she would first have to renew her Bronze Medallion qualification to meet the requirements. It had been many years since she'd been qualified and knew that the lifesaving procedures had changed drastically. So that's where she started. She was pleased to learn that her Bronze Medallion lessons were available on Thursday nights, so Russ would be home from work and could take care of the children.

'Russ, I need you to look after the kids while I take some swimming lessons every Thursday night.' she said.

'What do you need to take lessons for? You already know how to swim.' he said in surprise.

'It's to get my Bronze Medallion that will qualify me as a lifeguard.'

'What do you want to be a lifeguard for?' he enquired.

'That's not why I'm taking it. I have to have that qualification before I can obtain a swimming teaching licence.' she said calmly. She had the feeling that he was going to try to stop her from doing this.

'Why would you want to do that?' he asked angrily.

'I think it's about time I started living again and doing things that *I* like to do for a change.' she replied.

Russ thought it was a stupid idea and didn't support her in any way and said, 'Don't expect me to look after the kids every Thursday night while you're pursuing this stupid idea.'

Later, when she analysed his comments she realised that he was threatened by the fact that she would do something without consulting him first. Three times during the ten-week course Russ let her know at the last minute that he was going out that Thursday night. She had prepared for this eventually and had earlier confirmed that Denise

Evans from next door would be available on Thursday nights should she need her.

At her first lesson, Jenny and another woman began talking and hit it off right away. Little did Jenny know that this woman would eventually become her closest, lifelong friend. Marjorie Stewart's husband Darren had taught her boys hockey, so Jenny had met him many times, but had never met his wife Marjorie. They were pleased to learn that they both wanted to eventually become swimming instructors.

On the Monday, three days before Jenny was to challenge her Bronze Medallion swim test, she was shovelling the sidewalk at the side of her home when she fell heavily on the icy concrete. She felt something crack in her lower back and was in agony. She was terrified that she might again be paralysed, but upon checking her legs she realised that she still had feeling in them. But she winced at the sharp pain she felt in her lower back.

She glanced up at the living room picture window and could see that four-year-old Debbie had seen her fall. Jenny was concerned that she might come outside without her snowsuit.

Jenny rolled over and slowly and painfully crawled up the four stairs to the front door. Debbie's little face was full of concern.

'Mommy's okay sweetie.' Jenny said as she tried to reassure her.

'Why are you crawling, Mommy?' Debbie asked.

'My back is just very sore,' she said, and she kept crawling until she reached a telephone. She lay on her side as she spoke to Dr. Sims. He was able to see her right away. Although it was extremely painful, Jenny dressed Debbie and drove to the doctor's office.

After examining her Dr. Sims announced, 'You've fractured your tail bone.'

'How is that kind of fracture dealt with?' she asked.

'Well, we don't put you in a body cast or anything like that. There's nothing we can do but give you pain relief. It will be very painful for you to sit and lie on your back, so go to the pharmacy and buy a donut; that's a rubber disc that you blow up. Put it into a pillow case and use it to sit on. You will also find that you'll have to lie on your side when you sleep.'

'I have a swimming test Thursday night. Will it harm me if I have to get in the pool and rescue a victim?' she asked cautiously.

'No, you won't damage it any more than it is. But it will likely be too painful for you to do everything that's necessary to pass your exams. I'll give you a note explaining what happened, so maybe you can challenge the exam later.'

She walked next door to the pharmacy, filled the prescription and bought the donut. Before settling herself carefully in her car, she blew up the donut. It helped tremendously because it kept her sore tailbone from touching anything solid. It became her constant companion even in bed, and she carried it with her everywhere until the fracture was less painful.

It was so painful in bed that she decided she had better sleep alone rather than take the chance that Russ would bump her in any way. So she slept down in the rumpus room on a long sofa for the next three nights.

That Wednesday afternoon, she decided to go to the pool for a swim to see whether she'd be able to challenge the Thursday exam. She felt considerable pain but realised that she could do most of the things she had to do for her exam. She stubbornly didn't want to miss taking the test because she didn't want Russ to tell her 'I told you so.'

On Thursday night Russ looked incredulously at her when he saw her come into the kitchen carrying her swimming bag. 'You aren't going to do that test tonight are you?'

'I can't pass the test unless I try. So yes, I'm going to take the test.'

He just shook his head and she left for the pool. During the test she groaned when she saw that the supposedly 'unconscious' person she was chosen to save from the bottom of the deep end of the pool was the biggest man in the group. He was well over six feet tall and built like a football player. After retrieving him from the bottom of the pool, she would then tow him to the shallow end, somehow get him out of the water and give simulated mouth-to-mouth resuscitation. She wondered if she should back out of taking that part of the test but decided to at least try to do it.

Her heart was beating like a trip-hammer as she proceeded through the process. She took a deep breath and dove to the bottom of the pool. Then she struggled to bring her 'victim' to the surface. When they reached the surface, he was so big it was hard for her to get her arm across his chest to tow him. She was submerged several times as she struggled to get him to the shallow end of the pool. When she reached the end of the pool she knew it would be difficult getting him out of the water. She placed him parallel to the side of the pool and holding his head with her left hand she rolled his body with her right using the bottom of the pool as a solid base. Her 'drowning victim' gave a grunting noise as she did so. 'Oops,' she said quietly to the 'unconscious' man, 'I hope I didn't hurt you.' she whispered.

'I'm fine,' he whispered back.

Jenny did run into problems though when she attempted to give him simulated artificial resuscitation. She was supposed to rock from his head to his chest to check his breathing but was terribly worried that one of her heels would dig into her throbbing tailbone. When the examiner asked her why she was doing that step so awkwardly, she finally admitted to him that she had a fractured tailbone.

'You what!' he exclaimed. 'And you towed that huge man all that way with a fractured tailbone? My God woman, why didn't you tell me – I would have had you explain verbally what you would do.' Her 'victim' also shook his head in amazement. Jenny then went to her swimming bag and gave the examiner the copy of the letter from her doctor.

She was pleased to know that she would not be required to be a 'victim' in case the person 'saving' her bumped her tailbone.

When it came time to let the students know the results of their tests, Jenny was very pleased that he gave her an extra commendation because of her injury. The one that clapped the most was the man she had towed the length of the pool. Jenny clutched the document in her hands and just beamed. She felt such a sense of accomplishment.

Marjorie had also passed, so they knew they could both progress to the next stage of training towards becoming swimming instructors. They gave each other a big hug.

Suddenly two of the students threw the examiner into the pool then pushed each other in until the pool was full of students, instructors and the examiner. The only one who was not shoved into the pool was Jenny, so she made a shallow dive and got in herself – smiling as she surfaced beside the examiner. What a great and momentous night that had been!

When she arrived home from the pool she was bubbling over with excitement; she'd done it! She'd passed her exam with a fractured tailbone. As she tucked in her sons, Mark asked, 'Did you pass Mom?'

'I did!' she said proudly.

The children could see how excited she was and gave her a big hug. She kissed them goodnight and went into the living room where Russ was watching television. He continued watching television and never once either that night nor later, asked her whether she had passed her test.

Two weeks later she and Marjorie began their swimming instructor lessons. These were held on Wednesday nights, so again it was also convenient with Russ's schedule. Jenny made the same arrangements with Denise in case Russ refused to stay at home with the children.

She and Marjorie both earned their teaching licences and began working at the local pool as swimming instructors. Although Russ objected strenuously, Jenny worked two afternoons a week while the boys were at school. Agnes babysat Debbie while she was working. Occasionally she accepted evening classes while Denise watched the children.

Marjorie worked the full five-day week teaching school children how to swim. Her children were all in full-time school, so she was able to be home after school.

When the head instructor at the pool saw how competent Jenny was at teaching, she gave her three special groups to teach. The first was a group of adults who were quietly referred to as 'panic victims.' These were people who had suffered a traumatic experience associated with water and were terrified of it. Most hated getting their faces wet and some had taken two or three sets of ten lessons and were still terrified of water. Most were still determined to learn how to swim in case any of their children ran into trouble in the water.

Jenny solved some of their panic problems by being in the pool with them whenever they went into deep water. At the beginning of their first lesson, she had them stand along the side of the pool at the shallow end with their arms holding the side of the pool. Then she demonstrated how she wanted them to put their faces in the water and blow bubbles. At all times they would keep their feet on the bottom of the pool and their arms held securely onto the side of the pool. They were to practice this at home for the coming week until their next lesson.

'What I want you to do is fill your kitchen sink with water and practice this in the safety of your own kitchen. Do it at least twice a day, making sure of course that you have a towel to dry off after you have done it. For those of you who work during the day, do it before you have your shower in the morning and possibly again in the evening some time.'

At their second lesson they were asked to pick a black hockey puck off the shallow end of the pool. Most tried but couldn't reach it by just bending down.

'Why do you think you can't pick it up?' Jenny asked.

'I guess we have to get our feet off the ground to get it.' one portly student replied.

'I think I might have to push myself with my feet to get down there.' replied a petite mother of two.

'I guess I will have to get my face wet.' answered another.

'What do you think is keeping you from getting the puck?' Jenny asked.

The answer was shoulder shrugging.

'The reason you can't pick it up is because you have two balloons keeping you at the top of the water. Those balloons are called lungs. Whenever they're full of air they usually float you to the top of the water. If you panic however, you may blow out all your air and can sink in the water.'

She watched them nod their heads. 'Men have more difficulty with buoyancy than women because they have more muscle mass than women. Women on the other hand have more subcutaneous tissue; fat. Sorry ladies, that's the truth, but it does help you float easier than men.'

They all laughed, and she went on. 'There are enough pucks at the bottom of the pool for all of you. I'll show you how you'll have to push yourself down to the bottom of the pool, so you can reach the puck.'

Jenny demonstrated how to do this then added, 'Now one at a time, I'd like each of you to pick up a puck. Who wants to go first?'

They all had a try, and some were surprised that even though they thought they'd pushed themselves down enough to grab a puck; they floated to the top before they could reach it. If anyone seemed to be floundering Jenny righted the person until the student had his or her feet securely on the bottom again. They practiced this for the next fifteen minutes until they felt comfortable diving down and getting their bodies fully submerged.

The next week, while they stood at the side of the pool, she had them practice holding their breath. Using a timer, she was able to let them know that holding their breath for a minute was not difficult. Then she had them jump one at a time into deep water.

'Most of you will be able to hold your breath for well over a minute. So, don't panic when you jump in. You will pop back up to the surface in well under a minute, so won't need another breath for some time. By the time you need a breath, your lungs will have brought you up to the surface.'

They were instructed to take a deep breath and jump, then relax and let themselves float to the surface. They knew Jenny was nearby in the water if they had any problems.

When they had all done this a few times, they all cheered at each other. Most of them never thought they would be able to master their fear of water. By the end of ten lessons, Jenny had them jumping off the low diving board and swimming across the deep end of the pool.

Her second special group was toddlers; most of them being three- and four-year-olds with three to five in each class. She called them her 'tadpoles.' Most Canadian children did not obtain swimming lessons until they were in school, but the swimming pool where she taught believed that children should learn to get used to water when they were toddlers.

Whenever they were in the water they wore special floatation jackets that had been hand made by the instructors. These harnesses were circular bands of cotton fabric that had pockets all around the device that held pieces of Styrofoam. The circular bands were clipped together at the back of the child with big plastic clips. Straps were sewn to the circular band to fit over the child's shoulders that would keep the floatation device securely held around the child. As the child became more and more confident in the water, lighter Styrofoam pieces were inserted, or some pieces were removed, until the child was able to swim without any floatation assistance.

The pool officials seriously advised the parents not to use the little blow-up arm flotation devices because they could easily slide off the child's arms. The paramount rule was never to leave children unattended in a pool.

Jenny had fun working with the toddlers and before long had them jumping off the low diving board into the water. She was always there to see that they were fine once they bobbed to the surface and would watch them till they reached the side of the pool before the next toddler jumped.

The third group she taught were high school boys. Their regular instructor was away for several weeks, so Jenny took over their classes. At the first lesson, she asked them to swim four lengths of the pool using four different strokes. The boys did nothing but fool around; did not swim properly at all. After a few minutes she blew the whistle, beckoned them out of the pool and had them congregate at the side of the pool. She decided she was going to teach them a different kind of lesson.

'What would you do if you came home from school, heard a scream and found your mother lying on the basement floor? She's had an electrical shock and isn't breathing.'

They all shrugged their shoulders.

'How many of you have young brothers and sisters?'

Several raised their hands.

'What would you do if you found him or her floating face down in a wading pool or lying with a plastic bag over his or her head? He or she's not breathing.'

'What would you do if you found your father lying on the living room floor? He's had a heart attack and is not breathing.'

Again, they shrugged their shoulders, but their faces showed that they were now listening carefully to Jenny.

'Well, for all of these situations you would have to know how to do artificial resuscitation and the steps to take for CPR, coronary pulmonary resuscitation. How many of you know how to do that?'

'I saw it demonstrated on television one day but can't say I really remember how it should be done.' replied one tall teenager.

'I'm going to teach you how to do it.' she said as she looked around the group.

She showed them how to do it then had them simulate the action without really breathing into the other's mouth or pushing hard on the chest. She commended them on paying such close attention to the lesson. Then Jenny noticed the head instructor watching her with the boys and when she was finished teaching them CPR, she quietly pointed out to the boys that the head instructor was watching. She said, 'I want you to show her how well you can swim. Now get back in the pool and do lengths of the four strokes you were supposed to do earlier, but this time do them properly!'

They all took off and really burned up the pool doing the four strokes. When they had finished, Jenny praised them on how well they had done during the entire lesson.

'Will you be our instructor next week?' one boy asked.

'I think your regular teacher will be away for a couple of weeks. But I hope you will all behave for her like you behaved for me, because there's a lot to learn about swimming that can save not only your own life but help you be strong enough to save someone else's.'

Later, the head instructor took Jenny aside and asked, 'What the devil did you say to those kids? They were very serious and not clowning around while you taught them CPR. How did you get them to do that? And they really burned up the pool at the end of the lesson.'

'I just gave them all a scare showing them they weren't prepared, should they run into anyone, especially a family member who isn't breathing and will likely die without their help.'

After that, Jenny was given regular teen classes to instruct. Word got around at the school and both male and female students asked whether she could be their instructor. Jenny's self-esteem rocketed. She had made the right decision by getting her swimming instructor's license.

Chapter 33

One morning Jenny received a phone call from Mr. Gordon, the principal of Bruce's school. He explained that Bruce was having problems at school and asked if there were any problems at home. Jenny explained that she and her husband were having marital problems and that it likely was affecting Bruce more than she realised. Mr. Gordon suggested that Bruce might improve if he obtained counselling. He also suggested that Jenny see a marriage counsellor.

'My husband and I have already been to a counsellor and he refuses to go again. Our marriage is falling apart anyway. Do you have someone you can recommend who can help Bruce? she enquired.

'There's a counsellor I'd like to recommend who's had tremendous success with one of our other students.'

That night Jenny sat down beside Russ as he watched TV. 'I have something to discuss with you. Mr. Gordon, the principal at Bruce's school has told me that Bruce is having problems at school. His grades are plummeting, and he's had several fights with other students. He's suggested that we take him to a school counsellor to see if one can help him.'

Ross shook his head in exasperation and almost shouted as he replied, 'There's nothing wrong with that kid! He just needs a clip on the ear, so he'll behave better.'

Jenny just shook her head at his attitude and left the room. She didn't think Russ really cared about the trouble Bruce was in and seemed oblivious to the tension that was part of their every-day lives. The next morning, she made an appointment with a student counsellor knowing full well that Russ would not approve.

With her new sense of confidence, Jenny felt she had every right to make such decisions without his approval. No longer was she going to allow Russ to bully her into giving in to his wishes.

Two days later she collected Bruce at school and took him to the school counsellor. The counsellor, a child psychiatrist, ushered Bruce into his office and after he had spoken with Bruce, he walked with him into the waiting room. He gestured to Jenny and said, 'I'd like a few minutes of your time.'

He leaned across his desk, a concerned look on his face and said, 'If it's possible for you to do so, try to reduce the amount of friction that's in your home. Both you and your husband need to be patient while Bruce is going through this hard time. I've prescribed a mild sedative that should help him sleep and keep him on a more even keel. I'd like to see him next week to see if things have improved. '

That evening, Jenny spoke to Russ after the children were asleep. She knew he would be upset with her; that he didn't believe the boy had emotional problems. 'Russ, I took Bruce to the school counsellor today. He says Bruce is in trouble emotionally because of the tension between you and me. We've got to lessen the tension between us or he's not going to improve. To get him through this rough time, he's prescribed a mild tranquiliser.'

Russ looked up from his newspaper with a scowl. 'There's nothing wrong with Bruce. It's you who should be on tranquilisers. You're the crazy one!' he exclaimed.

Jenny gasped, then said what had been on the tip of her tongue for months, 'Well, it doesn't seem as if there's anything left of our marriage. You don't care about me, and now it's obvious that you don't care about the welfare of Bruce either. I want a divorce.'

Russ didn't seem surprised at her outburst. He slammed down his newspaper and pointed as he said, 'There's the front door and there's the back. Take your pick.'

'You know I don't have any money. Where would we go?' she asked anxiously.

'That's your problem. I'm not leaving!' he said as he stormed out of the room.

They had been married for thirteen years, and Jenny couldn't believe she'd finally had the courage to take the step she knew was coming for many years. However, in the next few days she faced unexpected resistance from Russ. She soon recognised that although he didn't appear to want her, he didn't want her to walk out on him either.

Because of Bruce's emotional problems she knew it would be better if Russ left their home, so decided to try and stick it out until he did.

Not being able to afford a lawyer, she contacted the Legal Aid Society. They appointed a lawyer to help her obtain first a legal separation, then a divorce. Jenny hoped it wouldn't take too long and that Russ would be forced to leave. Her lawyer did not give her much hope that he would be forced to do so, but Jenny was glad she'd begun the long process towards being free of Russ and his dominance in their lives.

Three days after she had told Russ she wanted a divorce, Jenny went to the bank to withdraw some money for groceries and clothing for the children. The account was closed. Russ had closed their joint account and had opened another in just his name the day after she'd asked him for a divorce.

'How was he allowed to do that?' she asked the teller, 'It was a joint account! Shouldn't he have had to get my permission to remove the money?'

'No, you both had signing authority on the account.' replied the teller.

As she left the bank empty handed, she pondered, 'What am I going to do? I have no money. Russ likely thinks that it will be impossible for me to move out if I don't have money to live on. But what am I going to do? I don't want to go to my parents for help again.'

Then she realised that she still had her credit card and hoped that Russ hadn't closed that as well, so at the grocery store, she filled her basket with essential items and went to the checkout counter. When she presented her credit card, the clerk asked whether she wanted some extra cash. Jenny shrugged her shoulders and decided, *"What the hell – all they can do is refuse it."*

'Can you make that an extra hundred dollars?' she asked.

Jenny held her breath while the clerk processed her credit card and breathed a sigh of relief when it was accepted. At least she had that way of paying for things she and the children might need. Then she went to the department store and bought the children new runners and clothes that she had planned to buy for them with the credit card. She wanted to keep the cash for transactions that were too small to use the credit card such as the children's lunch money and allowances.

Later, when the credit card bills came in, she hid the invoices from Russ and paid the minimum amount with the extra cash she withdrew on the card. Russ didn't seem to be worried about where Jenny had obtained the money. Jenny thought that Russ likely thought she'd received the money from her parents.

Chapter 34

During the next three months, Jenny carefully examined Russ's past behaviour. She knew she'd felt terribly depressed and unhappy during most of her marriage but always believed that it was something in herself that caused her unhappiness. However, after Reverend Thompson explained that what Russ was doing to her was a form of wife abuse, she spent considerable time at the library researching the topic.

The books about spousal abuse opened her eyes. Not only did they identify the signs that pointed to abuse and how to deal with it, but most advised that it was best for the person to leave the abusive relationship. She recognised that Russ was guilty of doing many abusive things both before and after she'd asked him for a divorce.

Jenny learned that abusive men were often oblivious to the sexual needs of their partners and meeting their own sexual needs was all that was important. Abusive men also fail to recognise the signs when other men abused their wives or others. For instance, he refused to step in when his friend Grant had hurt Betty, his pregnant wife. He also ignored the fact that Barry, their older neighbour was abusing his own wife, Jenny. In fact, he thought Barry's actions were funny and did not think it was necessary to defend Jenny against his actions.

Abusive men keep their wives financially dependent. Jenny had to account for every penny she spent and was not allowed to have an income or separate bank account of her own. Russ wanted Jenny to stay home with their children, so she was not allowed to work even though she wanted to. When Jenny defied him and took a part-time job to earn money one Christmas, he made it clear that she was still responsible for the complete care of the home and their children and their babysitting costs would come out of her salary.

Abusive men isolate their wives from others. Slowly, but surely Jenny's friends drifted away, because Russ would not socialise with them. He had few friends of his own, so she was very lonely. Russ made it clear that his job was to work and hers was to stay home and look after their home and children. She had the full responsibility for the care and upbringing of their children.

Not only had Russ abused her, but Jenny realised that Russ abused his children as well. He almost ignored them when he was home. He rationalised this by saying he would spend more time with them when they were older.

The only time Russ interacted with Debbie was to spoil her and give her anything she wanted even though Jenny had forbidden it. This left Debbie confused about what she was or wasn't allowed to do.

Russ took delight in encouraging the boys to fight and wrestle with each other. Although Bruce was younger by sixteen months, he and Mark were often asked whether they were twins. Bruce was as big and as heavy as Mark. While Mark's personality was more intellectual; Bruce's was more of a rough-and-tumble style than intellectual. Mark liked learning and reading. Bruce enjoyed roughhousing and being active. It was obvious to Jenny that Mark hated it when his father insisted that they fight. When Mark was older, he refused to fight saying, 'Why would I want to fight with Bruce. He's my brother. I don't want to hurt him, and I don't want him to hurt me just for nothing!' and he walked away.

Russ then called him a sissy because he wouldn't fight.

Instead of being with his children, Russ spent his time puttering with his tools in his basement workshop or working on patrol with the guard dogs. Although he could have worked a day sift at the railway with weekends off, he decided that Wednesday and Thursday were the nights he wanted off. So the children were in school during the week and he was not home except for Wednesday and Thursday evenings. On Saturday and Sunday when the children were home he ignored them as usual, then headed off to work later in the day.

Russ's shiftwork left Jenny at home on the weekends when most couples were socialising with each other. Russ and Jenny's social life was almost non-existent, but when they did go out, it was to his choice of tavern that had a live band. Most of the people got up to dance. Russ knew that Jenny loved to dance, but she was forced to sit and watch everybody else dancing because he refused to do so. If she danced with other men, he would be calm at the tavern, but took out his rage on her later by forcing her to have very rough sex.

Once Jenny recalled telling him, 'I would never think of taking you to a restaurant and not allowing you to eat. That's the same as you taking me some place where people are dancing and you won't dance. That's a form of torture to me. You can dance but refuse to do so.'

When Jenny asked for a divorce, Russ refused to leave the home. So, Jenny moved into her sons' room and put the boy's beds in the rumpus room downstairs. One day when she was getting an outfit out of their master bedroom closet, she noticed a rifle leaning against the wall. She identified it as the rifle the police had confiscated for three months when Russ had been hunting illegally at night.

Russ knew she was deathly afraid of rifles or guns of any kind and Russ normally stored the rifle at Antonio's home. She checked and saw that it was fully loaded. *"How dare he leave a loaded gun in the house within reach of the children!"* she thought angrily.

She carefully removed the clip then looked around wondering what she should do with the bullets. She knew she couldn't just put them into the garbage, so looked around the yard. Grabbing a shovel, she buried the clip deeply in a corner of the back garden beside Thor's kennel. The next week she checked the rifle and was angered to see that it was again loaded. She repeated her earlier action and buried the clip in the garden knowing that Russ was doing this to scare her into leaving their home.

When she found the rifle fully loaded a third time, her mind snapped. Instantly, she was in a blind rage and decided that when Russ came home in two hours, she was going to finish him off with his own rifle. How dare he treat them this way? The children would still be at school, so they were safely out of the way. She sat on the bed holding the rifle and started rehearsing in her head how she would do it. Would she just wait till he came in the door and let him have it, or would she allow him to explain why he had endangered his children so severely. Then she realized that he would just try to talk her out of it and would likely be able to overpower her before she had the courage to follow through with her threat.

So, she decided she would blast him as soon as he got home. He would come in the back door with the groceries, so she would hide in the living room. She even visualized him falling to the floor with his blood spattered all over the wall behind him. This vision so appalled and shocked her that she dropped the rifle then immediately gasped when she recognised that it could have gone off when she'd dropped it.

She was trembling all over so went to the kitchen and made herself a cup of tea to calm herself down. Then she re-thought what she was planning to do and knew that she wasn't capable of killing her children's father. But what was she to do? She started by unloading the rifle and buried the bullets in the back yard as before.

When she returned to the house, she was still blindingly furious with Russ for doing this to her and his children – so mad that she did something that she would never have contemplating doing if she hadn't been pushed the breaking point. After returning to the bedroom, she grabbed the rifle, stomped down the stairs to Russ's basement workroom and went on a rampage. She picked up a sledgehammer and smashed the rifle into a hundred pieces, then looked over at Russ's workbench. There, where it had been for four months, was the vacuum cleaner that Russ had promised to fix. When it was smashed to pieces, she did the same to all the other items he'd promised to fix for her. When her rage was over, she lowered the hammer and surveyed the mess. Her rage had gone, and she knew that Russ would not be able to leave the loaded rifle in their home again. Then she left the room and all its mess for him to find. He never commented about the mess – just left it where it was.

One night, after she'd asked him for a divorce, Russ came home from work well after midnight. It was obvious from the noise he was making that he'd been drinking. He turned the stereo on full blast, which woke the entire family. When the boys came upstairs, he shouted at them to get back to bed, and finally went into the master bedroom and collapsed on the bed. Jenny got up and turned the stereo off and went downstairs to comfort the boys.

Another night reeking of alcohol, he came into Jenny's bedroom and tried to force her to have sex. Jenny had been asleep but fought him off when she realised what he was trying to do. However, she had little success at repelling him because he now weighed two hundred and thirty pounds. She twisted and turned trying to fight him off, knowing she had to be quiet otherwise the children might wake up.

Mark, who was then eleven, was sleeping in the basement with Bruce. Somehow, he heard her struggles and came upstairs with a golf club in his hand, ready to hit his father. Jenny saw him over Russ's shoulder and yelled, 'No Mark, don't!' Russ turned around and glared at Mark.

Jenny said, 'Look at what you're doing to your children. You should be ashamed of yourself!' Russ got up, staggered past Mark and slammed the bedroom door so hard the entire neighbourhood must have heard it. Mark started to sob, and Jenny held him and hugged him. 'Thanks for being there Mark.'

They heard another door bang and realised that Russ had left their home. Jenny took Mark downstairs and put him to bed. When she returned to her room, she propped a chair against the door in case Russ tried again. She heard him come in again an hour later, but he went directly to the master bedroom where he slept.

Chapter 35

The day after Russ tried to rape her, Jenny decided that drastic action was needed. She could no longer wait for Russ to move out. Russ's behaviour was deteriorating to a dangerous level, and she had to get away from him to protect not only herself but her children as well.

Because Russ kept obtaining continuances for the separation to be finalised, Jenny was afraid that he would learn about her use of the credit card. Her car was so old that she knew it wouldn't last long, so she knew she had some big expenses coming up. So, she decided to speak to the welfare people to see if they could help her out financially until Russ was forced to support them. She made an appointment and when they called her name, she left the children in the waiting room. Her caseworker was Sally McCormack and Jenny liked her right away. Sally could see how stressed Jenny looked and had seen her lovely well-behaved children sitting in the waiting room. 'What do you want us to do to help you?'

'I've asked my husband for a divorce and want to stay in my home, but my husband refuses to leave. I'm really worried about my son Bruce. He's obtaining counselling and is in bad emotional shape because of the tension in our home. His doctor has advised me not to work until Bruce is better. I've lost ten pounds in three months and I can't afford to lose any in the first place.'

'Well then, I guess you'll need an alternative place to live in. Would you like me to see if I can arrange that?' she asked.

Jenny knew that she couldn't withstand much more tension and knew that Bruce and the other children couldn't either, so she agreed to have her arrange for alternative accommodations. Jenny knew she would likely have to live in a place far below the standards of the children's present home but felt it would be worth it. Then another thought occurred to her, 'But how will I move there?'

'We'll provide a moving van to move you there.' Sally explained.

'And we won't have any money to buy groceries and things the children need for school. How will I pay for those kinds of expenses?' she said wringing her hands.

'We'll give you a monthly allowance for necessary expenses.' Sally added.

Jenny couldn't believe that this was finally happening; that she was finally able to leave Russ. She breathed a big sigh of relief. 'Could you arrange all that for me please?'

'We'll do everything we can to expedite this. I know of a place that was available a few days ago. Let me check to see if it's still available.'

'Oh yes. Please do. The sooner we move the better.' Jenny added excitedly.

Within less than a week all the arrangements had been made. Russ had been in the habit of driving directly to their cottage at the lake after his Tuesday four-to-twelve shift and normally didn't come back until the morning of Friday to be ready for his next shift. Before leaving for work on the Tuesday nights he began loading a trailer with furniture from their rumpus room to take to the lake. The first Tuesday, he took the sofa set Jenny had recovered then took the end tables that matched it the week after. The next of his weekends, he took an old beer fridge. Jenny began to wonder if he was planning to move down to the cottage but knew she couldn't take the chance that this was not his plan.

So, because he would likely be gone from Tuesday till Friday as usual, Jennie decided that the best time for her to have the moving truck come was the next Wednesday morning. Sally confirmed the arrangements and for the rest of the week Jenny began secretly packing boxes and hiding them in the children's closets. She stored a bunch of empty boxes at her brother Jeff's home. Her father had agreed to come and help her move, so flew in on Tuesday morning. Jeff picked him up at the airport and drove him over to

Jenny's at four o'clock after Russ had gone to work. He brought the extra boxes with him then took Debbie back with him so Jenny, the boys and her father could get on with the packing.

Jenny hadn't told the boys what was going on until their grandfather arrived. She explained the situation to Mark and Bruce and they began packing boxes of toys and clothes from their bedroom. They seemed relieved that they would be getting away from Russ and soon.

By ten o'clock, the boys were so tired they were weaving on their feet. Jenny sent them to bed and she and her father continued packing until all the boxes were filled. They knew they would need more boxes, so her dad took Jenny's old car and drove behind the local grocery store and scavenged the boxes that were in a bin at the back.

By the time the moving truck arrived at eleven the next morning, they had finished breakfast and had packed all the rest of the bedding and belongings.

Jenny didn't feel guilty about taking the furniture because most of it was hers anyway. She had bought the bedroom suite in the master bedroom, the kitchen table, the living room suite and the carpet in the living room with her own money. Over the years, on special occasions such as birthdays and Christmas, Russ did not give Jenny personal gifts. Instead he gave her appliances, so she felt these were hers as well. He'd given the refrigerator to her one birthday, the washer and dryer he'd given to her for Christmas. The same went for her toaster, her kettle and television.

When Jenny arrived at the new townhouse she was amazed at how nice it was. She'd expected a run-down place, but this one was brand new. She looked around and marvelled at their new spacious kitchen, dining and living room that were on the main floor. There was a small bathroom off the kitchen that she knew would be handy for them all.

Upstairs, there were three bedrooms. The boys as usual would be sharing a bedroom, but Jenny gave them the master bedroom, so they would have more room. The boys were finally able to put their single beds side by side instead of having them set up as bunk beds. They loved their new bedroom. Jenny didn't need much room herself so settled herself in one of the smaller bedrooms.

The only concern she had was that there was mud everywhere. The sod still hadn't been laid, nor had any of the greenery been planted.

Just after dinner, Jeff delivered Debbie and she loved her little room and promptly got busy unpacking her toys. It wasn't long before her head was drooping, and her grandpa helped her put on her pyjamas and she dozed off in her new bedroom, her favourite teddy clutched in her arms.

A few days later, Martha arrived driving her little Austin 1100. She'd driven all the way from Victoria, so was very tired. She was pleased to see that Jenny and the children had such a nice home. Ian and Martha stayed for a week, and when they were leaving, her mother asked Jenny to hold out her hand. In it she placed the keys for her Austin and the registration slip showing that Jenny was now the owner of the car.

'We can't bear the thought of you driving that old relic any more. We want you to have a car that's reliable.' explained Martha.

Jenny's looked incredulously at Martha then burst into tears. 'How am I ever going to pay you back for all the kind things you've done for us?'

'You'll find a way in the future somehow. But don't worry about it. Your Dad and I have another car at home and because we're retired, we really don't need two cars. I didn't want to see you doing without a car. I'm sure you and the children will make good use of it.'

That evening, her parents flew back to Victoria. After she and the children had driven them to the airport and the children were in bed, Jenny looked around her new home and felt such a sense of peace she burst out crying with the joy of it. She felt as if she had escaped from jail and had a sense of freedom she hadn't felt in years.

Her parents had been so good to her. One thing that always puzzled Jenny was why they had not spoken to her about their concerns about the cultural differences between her and Russ. They had never talked to her about it and she wondered if things would have been different if she had been warned before her marriage. If they had discussed their concerns with her, would she have picked up and confirmed those differences simply by watching the interaction between Russ's father, mother and brother? Would she have noticed how Russ gave in to his father's wishes? In hindsight, she wished that her parents had spoken up. On the other hand, she would not have her children, so some good came from their union.

So they settled into and loved their new home. It wasn't long before the sod was laid, and the greenery planted. In fact the landscape men let Mark and Bruce help plant some of the flowers. Life was good!

Chapter 36

Jenny hadn't realised how much pressure she and the children had been under when they lived with Russ – how the children had to watch that they didn't anger Russ. The change in their behaviour was remarkable. They squabbled less, slept better and seemed to enjoy life far more. And they smiled more. Even though they were dirt poor, they managed to be happy.

After Jenny was settled in her new home, she decided it was time to phone her friends and former neighbours to let them know how to get in touch with her. She needed a support group to help her through this difficult time. What she needed were others to believe in her and understand her, but she was sadly disappointed to learn who were and were not true friends.

What hurt Jenny the most was that Doreen and Hugh did not stick by her and wouldn't visit her when she invited them to see her new home. Her former neighbours Agnes Evans and Sarah, who she'd helped during the terrible storm, did not come to visit. Jenny felt very isolated from her friends.

The two people that stuck by her were Marjorie Stewart and Elaine Harrington. If it hadn't been for their support, Jenny would have felt totally deserted by those she thought were her friends. Elaine and Tom came over often and once Elaine held out her hand to display her engagement ring.

Marjorie couldn't do enough for her and helped her through the tough transition. Jenny blessed the day that she'd met her at her swimming class. Marjorie encouraged Jenny to continue teaching swimming and they often met for coffee and chats. One day when Jenny was a bit low about the desertion of her friends, Marjorie said, 'You've learned an important lesson. You've learned who your real friends are. Some never learn that important lesson, but they've shown their true colours by their desertion of you.

Remember, life is tough, but you're even tougher. You'll do fine.'

One morning when Jenny woke up she decided some changes were required now that she was heading towards single life. Russ had always insisted that she wear her hair long. She had hard-to-manage hair and this involved a lot of extra effort - effort she felt could be better spent enjoying life. His insistence on her keeping it long had always gnawed at her and she felt annoyed every time she had to fuss with her hair. One of the first things she did when she and the children were on their own was to go to a hairdresser and get her hair cut short into a pixie cut. Because she had small delicate features, the style suited her to perfection. She felt even more free from Russ, because now she could just 'wash and wear' her hair without the constant fussing. This proved a boon to her when she went back to teaching swimming.

Jenny had little money to spend on entertainment for herself and her children, but soon she found many places where she could take the children that didn't cost much money.

They found a small man-made lake not far from their home and spent many a day enjoying the water and the sunshine. They drove to Lower Fort Garry, to the Lockport Dam and attended several free concerts. Because they lived near the Assiniboine Downs racetrack, she made a point of taking the children there on 'Ladies' Day.' Jenny didn't believe in gambling but did love horses. Because children got in free, it was a lovely inexpensive evening for them all. Their treat of a hot dog and soft drink capped the evening. They didn't bet of course, but they did pick their favourite horse before each race and had fun when their pick turned out to win. It was a lovely summer and that fall the boys enrolled in a nearby school. Mark was in grade six and Bruce was in grade four.

Both boys were paperboys and made their pin money that way. One day Bruce came home with his face scratched and bleeding. 'What happened?' Jenny asked in concern.

'Kevin and Billy Watson pushed me off my bike while I was delivering papers. Because I had just picked up my newspapers, it was awkward to ride my bike and I got tangled up in it when I fell. But I gave one of the boys a good bash, but the other one grabbed my face and scratched it.' he said as he pointed to his bleeding face.

'Where do these boys live?' she asked.

'They live in our complex – in number 34.'

'Well, I'll speak to their parents. They're nothing but bullies.' she said emphatically.

After she cleaned up his face, she took Bruce with her and left Mark with Debbie. She knocked on the door of unit 34 and a rather shabbily dressed woman answered the door, wiping her hands as she came. 'Yes?'

Jenny explained what had happened. 'Oh, so he's the bully that bashed my boy!' she yelled.

'No. Your two boys pushed Bruce off his bike when he was delivering his newspapers.' As she spoke she could see two boys standing behind the woman. They were obviously one or two years older than her boys.

She continued, 'Then they started hitting him and Bruce fought back. But look at the dirty fighting your son's use – two against one and they're both older than Bruce. Look at how they scratched his face.' she said as she pointed to Bruce's cheek.

'Well, I still think it's your boy that started the fight.' she said as she stood with her hands on her hips.

'It was still two against one – surely you can't condone that kind of behaviour.' Jenny enquired.

The woman backed up and slammed the door. Jenny realised that the woman was not going to back down and she was wasting her time trying to reason with her. 'The apples didn't fall far from that tree.' she thought.

As they walked back to her home Jenny asked Bruce, 'Are you sure that's the way it happened?'

Bruce looked her in the eye and said, 'Yes, Mom. I'm not lying. That's how it happened.'

When Jenny got home she took her boys aside and spoke to them. 'It looks like the neighbour boys are street fighters and fight dirty. From now on, I want you both to deliver your newspapers, but together. Once you've delivered one set then deliver the other one. That way you'll be together, and they can't gang up on you. Okay?'

Both boys nodded.

'And another thing – with these boys only, you have my permission to bash them back. Someone has got to teach them a lesson and if you two are together, they won't be able to gang up on you.'

That evening Mark and Bruce practiced how they would fight back should the boys start trouble. 'The most important thing we have to do is to get off our bikes, so they can't tip us over.' said Mark.

Two days later, the inevitable happened. The Watson boys started trouble again. 'Sissy, sissy, sissy.' they chanted to Bruce. 'Had to get your mother to fight for you – what a sissy!' they taunted.

'Well it won't happen again.' said Bruce as he placed his bike on the ground.

'Oh yeah!' shouted Kevin and threw a fist at Bruce. This time Bruce was ready and dodged the punch but grabbed him around the neck and threw him to the ground.

Billy tried the same tactic with Mark, and also ended up on the ground. Both Bruce and Mark landed two-fisted punches and the Watson boys suddenly realised that they couldn't intimidate these two younger boys. They ran off holding their faces and tummies.

'And don't come back!' shouted Bruce, the more pugnacious of the two.

They had no more problems from the two bullies except for dirty looks any time they saw each other. In time, Mark and Bruce were able to deliver their newspapers alone again.

Jenny too was earning money. She worked part-time as a swimming instructor at the local Civic Centre. Marjorie Stewart was often working at the same time, and they enjoyed each other's company.

Jenny learned that a neighbour in the complex had a small crank-up tent trailer for sale for only seven hundred dollars. The family needed to buy a larger one for their expanding family and were only offered five hundred for it in trade. It slept four, so would be perfect for Jenny's family to use for camping. Jenny enquired and learned that her little Austin would not have trouble pulling it because of its low pulling weight. But how was she going to pay for it?

'I don't have that kind of money. Could I pay for it a bit every month?' she asked the owner.

'Maybe we can make a deal.' the woman replied, 'I have two girls that need care before and after school. Would you be interested in looking after them in exchange for buying the trailer? We'd be willing to pay you ten dollars an hour to do so.'

'You've got yourself a deal.' replied Jenny as she accepted the keys for the trailer. Because they would require a stronger hitch for their new trailer the husband installed their old one on Jenny's Austin. So they were all set for summer fun!

That summer they drove to many lakes where they could swim and enjoy their holidays. The boys were especially fond of the breakfasts of bacon and eggs that Jenny made on their little barbeque. They all had sleeping bags, but Jenny's and Debbie's could be zipped together to form a double sleeping bag.

Chapter 37

Jenny had befriended the resident manager of the complex, Doris Lockheart and they often had coffee together. One day Doris asked Jenny to accompany her while she was doing a regular three-month inspection of one of the units in the complex that was occupied by another welfare family.

'Why do you need someone to come with you?' Jenny asked.

'One of their neighbours said that unusual things are going on in that home and have encouraged me to do the inspection. I thought having a witness might be a good idea. Will you come with me as a witness?'

'Sure.' Jenny agreed.

When they entered the home, Jenny detected a terrible smell. It was autumn and the heat was on in the homes. When they entered the dining room, she and Doris just stood with their mouths open. There was a garden growing in the room! The family had brought buckets of earth into the dining room and had planted vegetables across the entire room.

'You can't do that!' Doris admonished the woman.

'Why not?' asked the woman. 'In my country we have gardens in our home.'

'Well, not here you don't. You'll first have to remove all the produce and earth and if you've damaged the flooring you will have to pay the cost of replacing it.'

The woman just shook her head.

Jenny spotted one of her many children squatting over a heat duct in the living room and saw him defecating into it. She motioned to Doris and she just shook her head.

'What is that child doing?' Doris asked.

'What does it look like he's doing?' asked the woman.

'Doesn't he know that there's a bathroom where he's supposed to do that?'

The woman just shrugged her shoulders. It suddenly became clear why the home smelled like a sewer.

'I'm going to have to report these things to the welfare people. That's a completely unacceptable way of using a home. You obviously don't know how to live in a nice home.'

When Doris returned to her office, she called the welfare people to tell them what had happened and requested that the family be removed immediately. They were assured that they would be moved to another home and given the rules of proper behaviour in those homes. They would also look after any repairs that would be necessary to bring the unit back to suitable health standards.

When Doris inspected the vacant home the next week, she realised that she was going to have to hire a crew of people to make the home habitable for anyone else. The plants and earth had to be removed and the dining room floor had to be replaced, as did all the pipes and air vents leading to the furnace. Upon inspecting the attic that had a crawlspace above the master bedroom, they found several used sanitary napkins. It took them three months of work and lots of airing out for the home to be habitable for another family.

Chapter 38

Jenny knew that when their divorce was granted, the proceeds from their home would be divided equally. However, she was astounded when she learned that every cent she'd received on welfare would come out of only her half of the property settlement. Russ still hadn't contributed a cent towards the children's upkeep and Jenny thought the welfare people should divide the children's expenses from both halves of the property settlement. After all, they were Russ's children too! Jenny also learned that Russ's new van and the summer cottage that she and Russ had built from scratch had been registered in Russ's name only, so she would receive nothing from them in the divorce settlement.

Since her children were born, Jenny had regularly deposited her government family allowance cheques into an account that was to be used for their education. Sadly, she was forced to start drawing from it, rather than use up too much of the equity from her half of the home.

Finally, a separation agreement was signed giving Russ Friday nights to see his children between six and ten o'clock. He was to pay only two hundred and twenty-five dollars a month towards child maintenance for his three children and one dollar per year alimony for Jenny.

Seventy-five dollars per child, thought Jenny, *"What a joke that was! The courts obviously were completely unaware of how much it cost to support a child. Nobody could possibly support a child on seventy-five dollars!"*

When Russ came to collect the children on his first visit, he just glared at Jenny. When the children were settled in his van, he came back to where Jenny was waving to the children. He glared at her as he spit venom at her, 'I have the home, the cottage, the van, the bank account and soon you'll have nothing.'

Then he stomped off to his car and drove away with the children. Later that evening she went over what Russ had said to her and realised that he had sworn a vendetta against her. "*How Italian.*" She thought. She worried the entire evening wondering if he was going to take off with the children and was relieved to see his van pull into the driveway at the appointed time.

In her regular letters to her parents, she told them what he had said. Ian and Martha warned her to be careful and if he didn't bring the children back at the appointed time, to call the police.

Jenny looked forward to her parent's letters. They swapped letters at least once a week and occasionally sent audio cassettes to each other. Martha began slipping the odd twenty-dollar bill into her letters and Jenny was able to buy a few treats for the family.

That winter, Jenny's little Austin got them around very well. One morning however, after it had been really cold overnight, she hadn't plugged it in soon enough. The car just coughed and chugged but wouldn't turn over. Her father had shown her a little screw she could turn that would enrich the fuel mixture. She lifted the hood, turned the screw and the car started just fine. Next, she returned the screw to where it would normally be. She had just closed the hood of the car when she heard a husky voice say, 'Could you do that to mine too?'

She looked up to see a neighbour approaching her. She laughed and raised the hood again and pointed to what she had done.

'Got it.' he said as he headed back to his car. Soon his car was purring, and he gave Jenny the thumbs up sign.

Chapter 39

Jenny was shopping one day six months after she moved out with the children. She turned her head when a woman called her name. Jenny recognised the woman as being the neighbourhood gossip from her old street.

'Did you know that Russ isn't living in your house any more and that he only comes there when he has the children on Friday nights?' she prattled.

'No, I didn't know that.' Jenny said and wondered whether the woman was getting a thrill passing on such a comment.

'Yeah. He's moved in with a woman and her daughter over on Market Street.'

'I see.' replied Jenny.

'Her name is Cloe Davis and her daughter's name is Maureen.' she added. They talked for a few minutes about what was happening in the old neighbourhood and Jenny continued her shopping.

'So, the home Russ forced me out of is vacant except when he visits with the children on Friday evenings.' she thought. 'I wonder if I could move back in now that he's not living there?'

Jenny was doing everything she could to obtain a divorce and was glad Russ had diverted his attention to another woman. It occurred to her she should warn the woman about him but didn't want to rock the boat. Also, because adultery was the only reason she could use to obtain a divorce from him, it would provide evidence that he was doing just that.

She considered moving back into their home, but her lawyer told her not to even consider the possibility of moving back because Russ would likely move back as well. Until the divorce and property settlement were finalised, this was not an option.

In the meantime, Jenny's social life improved. She'd joined an organisation called Parents Without Partners and soon had her own circle of friends. Most weekends they had dances and social get-togethers. Because Russ had the children on Friday nights for four hours, Jenny hired a babysitter to be there when they came home. She also hired the same babysitter if there were get-togethers on Saturday nights.

One Saturday night, Jenny had just left for an evening out when she noticed a familiar car in the parking lot of her townhouse complex. It belonged to Ron Baker, one of the young security police fellows she'd befriended. She went up to the car and as he rolled down the window, he sheepishly looked up at her. It suddenly dawned on Jenny, that Russ had hired him to follow her. 'Did Russ hire you to follow me?' she asked.

'You're not supposed to ask me that.' he said, but she knew that's exactly what was happening.

'Well here's the address where I'll be. I expect to be home shortly after midnight. Why not save yourself a lot of time and effort and just be here so I know I'll be safe when I get home?' she said as she took a piece of paper from her purse and wrote the address.

He just grinned sheepishly. He did follow her and parked outside the hall where the dance was being held. Jenny spoke about it to a couple of the people at the dance and they insisted that Jenny introduce them to her 'security squad.' She did, so she finally had witnesses to prove that Russ was having her followed. She asked the couple to write an affidavit stating what they had observed.

At one of the Parents without Partners meetings, she met Gordon Berry who was also separated from his wife. He really missed his children and was still fighting to have regular visitations with them. He met and hit it off with Jenny's three children. One summer day, Gordon asked whether she and the children would like to take a ride to Lockport, a small community located just north of the city of Winnipeg.

The boys were very excited to see Lockport and were ready to have fun that day. They were enthralled watching the locks work. Jenny packed a lunch and they enjoyed the afternoon walking around the area and having a picnic lunch. Having been there before, she knew there would be grassy hills the children could slide down, so she brought three flattened cardboard boxes.

Jenny smiled as she watched her children as they laughed and raced each other down the hill on their pieces of cardboard. It was good seeing them having so much fun. Just after five thirty Jenny called the children and told them it was time to go home. They begged for two more slides and she nodded. It was close to six o'clock by the time they left. Soon they were back at her home and she made dinner for them all. Gordon left when the children went to bed completely tired out from their busy afternoon.

That night as Jenny was watching the ten o'clock news she was horrified to hear the news report saying that just about the time they were leaving Lockport, a family of four in a canoe had attempted to go over the weir, but their boat had capsized. All four were subsequently rescued, but because nobody on shore knew CPR, two of them died.

'I was right there!' she almost screamed at the television. 'I could have saved them! Why oh why couldn't we have left fifteen minutes later!'

She phoned Gordon and told him the sad tale. He too knew CPR and they commiserated about why things happened the way they did in life. Both spent restless nights thereafter wondering what would have happened if they had still been there at the time the family had gone over the weir.

Chapter 40

One spring morning when Jenny left her home to drive to the swimming pool, she noticed that there was a scrape below the passenger window of the car and that the window was down. She knew she would never have left the window down in winter. She opened the door and tried to raise the window, but it wouldn't budge. Then she spied two of her audio cassettes on the floor of the car, so she knew someone had been in her car. Then Jenny remembered that she kept an extra house and car key under the dash of the car. She searched for them, but they were missing.

'This is serious.' she thought. 'I'll have to have the locks on my home changed right away.'

Jenny phoned Doris and she agreed to have a locksmith come right away. She wondered why the person hadn't driven the car away when they had a key. They obviously weren't interested in stealing the car but must have been after her house key. She was lucky the person didn't try to break in during the night. Then she remembered that both doors had dead bolts that she ensured were bolted every night before she went to bed. But she couldn't wait to get the locks changed in case the person tried to break in while she was out during the day.

The locksmith replaced the front and back door locks and Jenny felt relieved. He also had a look at the window of her car and was able to put it back on its track.

The next summer, Jenny decided she would try to rent a cottage at Grand Beach, her childhood summer place. She drove the car to the beach and asked at several places whether anyone knew where they could rent a cottage but had no luck. She sadly gave up and decided to drive home again, but before leaving the beach area, she and the children went into a restaurant that was at the top of a hill. They had lunch and when they returned to their car, it wasn't there. What she did see was a crowd of people at the bottom of the hill milling around a car that was resting against a big boulder. Her mouth open, she exclaimed, 'Oh my God! That's my car down there!'

She and the children ran down the hill. Jenny searched for any other vehicles that might have been hit by the car and was thankful to see that the car had not hit anything other than the huge boulder. How lucky that had been. It could have hit another car or a pedestrian. *"Someone has been looking after me today."* she thought.

When she got to her car she saw that the car was partially bogged down in the soft earth, so when it hit the boulder, it had slowed down considerably. The passenger's side of the car was dented slightly, but it looked as if it could be driven if a tow truck could move it away from the side of the big boulder.

Jenny knew that she'd locked the car and had put it into park, so this was no accident. She remembered the break-in she'd had a few months ago and couldn't help but think that whoever had stolen the key must have used it to get into her car today. She looked around but didn't recognise anyone. Because of the circumstances, she called the local police and a tow truck. The officer in charge took her statement.

'How did your car get here?' he asked.

Jenny pointed up the hill to where she had parked her car at the restaurant. 'I know I locked the car and had the parking brake on. I didn't know it had gone till we came out after lunch.' she said as she gestured to the children waiting in the shade under a tree.

'Then how did someone get into the car? It's unlocked.'

'I have no idea. However, my car was broken into a couple of months ago. I keep an extra key for my home and car hidden under the dash and both were missing. The person who found the key could have driven the car away at that time, but they didn't. I think they took the house key and might have planned to break in when it was vacant. I had the house locks changed the same day, but didn't think I needed to change the car locks.'

'Who do you think could have done that?' he asked.

'I don't really know. The only enemy I have is my ex-husband. He wasn't very happy when I left him. He has a cottage about ten miles away from here.'

'We'll investigate that. Sure was lucky for you, that the car didn't hit anyone on the way down.'

'That's for sure!'

The officer interviewed several of the bystanders to see if they had seen anyone near the car before it came down the hill. They all shook their heads. 'The first I saw of it was when someone yelled to watch out! Good thing they did, because it was heading right for me. I was able to get out of the way in time.'

The officer interviewed others at the parking lot at the top of the hill, but they too had not seen anyone around Jenny's car. While this was happening, the tow truck arrived, and the man was able to move the car sideways, away from the boulder. He examined the passenger side, opened and closed the doors, examined the wheel wells and was able to report that the only damage that would need to be repaired was a broken headlight and a dent in the passenger's door. He started the car, drove it a little way and said it was roadworthy. However, he admonished Jenny not to drive the car at night until the headlight was fixed.

The police never did catch whoever had sabotaged Jenny's car.

Later that year, Jenny and the children were going to a Halloween party sponsored by the Parents Without Partners Association. When Jenny looked out the window that morning, she saw that the snow that had been falling overnight was still falling and there were high drifts everywhere. Because they were on the outskirts of the city, the wind had drifted the snow so badly that she knew they wouldn't be able to get out of their complex until a snow plough came along. The children were very disappointed because they had been looking forward to going to the party and had worked hard on their costumes. Even Jenny had planned to wear one. They all had long faces during breakfast.

After breakfast, Jenny put on her winter parka and boots. 'I'll just be gone a few minutes.' she said.

She was back very soon and announced to the children, 'I think we can get out. Our car is so small, that it can go on the sidewalk. I've checked it out and we can get out of the complex to the street. It has already been ploughed, so we can go!'

They excitedly got into their costumes. Jenny went as a clown and had blackened several of her teeth and the children had a big laugh the first time she smiled at them. They all climbed into the car and prepared for the adventure of driving on the complex sidewalk. As they were driving carefully along the sidewalk, they received surprised looks from neighbours who were out shovelling their own walks. When Jenny smiled at them they all laughed too at her blackened teeth.

That day everyone was able to get out of the complex, except one of the neighbours who drove a van. It was too wide and too heavy and became completely bogged down and couldn't move further. So, Jenny had to park her car on the street for a few days until their parking lot was ploughed.

Chapter 41

Jenny knew that the only way she and Russ could get a divorce would be for her to charge him with adultery. She also knew that she would need concrete evidence to prove it.

It would cost a lot to hire a private detective to follow him. It went through her mind to contact Ron Baker from the security police firm but didn't want to put him in the middle of their situation. Her biggest problem was how to pay for a detective. Then her eyes spotted her diamond engagement and wedding rings. 'I wonder how much they would be worth?' she pondered.

That day she went to a pawnshop and learned that she would get five hundred dollars for the set and took the deal. Then she spoke with a detective who was recommended by one of her friends. She had been assured that the detective was good and didn't charge an arm and a leg. When she met him Jenny liked him immediately. He had a kind face and listened carefully as she told him her story. He probed for more details and Jenny could see that he was saddened by the problems her husband had caused her. 'Yes, I'll take the case.' he said. 'You can pay me on instalments if you need to, but I'm going to get this guy!'

He followed Russ for ten days and was able to establish that he was living with Cloe Davis and just went home to the matrimonial home on Friday nights when he had his weekly visit with his children.

At the beginning of June, Jenny and Russ went to court to settle their divorce. Jenny was very nervous being in the same room as Russ and when she had to testify she told the judge about the mental cruelty he'd submitted her to, his swearing of a vendetta against her, of having her followed when she went out socially and about how he had been living with another woman for over a year.

When Russ took the stand, he took out his security police notebook and started itemising the times Jenny had been out on evenings attending Parent's Without Partners meetings. He itemised the furniture she had taken from the home and how she had left very little for him. Jenny just sat shaking her head. 'How pathetic he is.' she thought.

Jenny's detective then submitted the testimony of the people who were witnesses to prove Jenny's allegations that Russ had hired security guards to spy on her. However, it was the detective's testimony proving that Russ spent his time living with another woman except when he saw his children that the judge approved of the divorce on grounds of adultery.

But Jenny was devastated when the Judge increased the time Russ would spend with the children by awarding him every second weekend with the children. He would pick them up on Friday evenings and bring them back on Sunday nights. After all those years at balking at doing so, Russ would have to change his days off from Wednesday and Thursday to Saturday and Sunday to be with his children.

Jenny was awarded half the property value of their home less the welfare payments that had been made to her and the children. Her portion of the marital home and property was only four thousand dollars – her half of the equity from the home after the welfare payments had been deducted.

'How ironic,' she thought, 'The equity I got from our home after fifteen years of marriage is the same amount of money I invested in our first home from the money I received in the settlement from my car accident. I was married to Russ all those years and came out without a cent extra from all that effort.'

She realised that she couldn't afford to buy Russ out so she could live in her former home. The thought of moving back there after the way her neighbours had deserted her, didn't make it a viable option anyway. Besides, after the welfare payments were deducted from her half of the property value, she would receive only four thousand dollars equity from the home. After the divorce, Cloe and Maureen moved in with Russ in Jenny's former home.

The detective sent Jenny his bill and she was overwhelmed to learn that he charged her only five hundred dollars.

Something Missing

Chapter 42

Bruce was still on medication and was doing much better at school. But suddenly a pattern of bad behaviour started re-occurring after their divorce. Bruce was wound up like a top when he returned home from his dad's visits on Sunday nights and remained difficult to handle until about Tuesday night every second week.

'What's going on Bruce,' Jenny asked.

'Nuthin.' was his reply.

She then asked Mark what he thought was causing his brother to be so badly behaved. 'Dad says he doesn't have to take his medicine, so Bruce doesn't take it on Saturday and Sunday when we're with Dad.'

Suddenly, things started to make sense. She called Russ and told him what she had found out. 'He doesn't need the medication – you do!' he said as he slammed down the phone.

So, Jenny had to struggle with Bruce's behaviour for two days out of every two weeks. She urged Bruce to keep taking his medication on the Saturdays and Sundays he was with his father. However, Bruce continued to have more and more bouts of bad behaviour.

The boys and Debbie were in the habit of getting up early to watch cartoons on the Saturday they were home with Jenny. Jenny was busy sorting the laundry when the angry shouting of her boys had her rushing downstairs. She arrived in the living room to see Bruce straddling Mark and pounding his fist into his brother's face. He was hitting him over and over until Mark's face was a bloody mess. She rushed over to Bruce to pull him off and was shocked by the almost insane look he gave her. As she pulled him away she wondered for a moment whether Bruce was going to hit her as well.

'Debbie, go next door to get Mrs. Henderson.' she said.

Their next-door neighbour was a nurse. She examined Mark, 'Jenny I think you should take him to emergency. He will likely need stitches to repair his torn upper lip.' As she examined him further, 'His teeth are all bloody, so he might lose a couple of teeth as well. There's also a tear in his tongue.'

She offered to stay with Bruce and Debbie while Jenny drove him to the hospital. At the hospital Mark had facial x-rays taken, then received four stitches to close the wound on his upper lip. When the x-rays were developed the doctor gave her the good news that his teeth would be all right and the small tear in his tongue would heal on its own.

Dr. Sims had been called and he also spoke with the emergency doctor. Then he asked Jenny to come with him into a private room. 'I'm really concerned that Bruce has gone off the rails so badly. Do you have any idea why that has happened after he's done so well on his medication?'

'His father refuses to let him take the medication when he's with him every second weekend. Bruce comes back so wound up that it takes me two days to get him back to normal. He's really under a lot of stress right now trying to please both his father and me. I think that's what's causing him to have more and more bad days.'

'I think it's time for him to see a psychiatrist again to see if there isn't some underlying problem that's causing this behaviour. In the meantime, I'd like to have Russ's phone number, so I can urge him to keep Bruce on his medication when he's with him.

'Would you arrange for the psychiatrist to see Bruce?'

'Yes I will, and my nurse will let you know when the appointment will be.'

Jenny took Mark home and put him to bed. The doctor had given her several painkillers to help him handle the pain during his first twenty-four hours. After Jenny had settled Mark, she spoke with Bruce. She was trembling with anger to think that Bruce had harmed his older brother so seriously.

'Bruce, why did you hurt Mark so badly?' she asked, trying to keep calm.

'He was teasing me about something.' he answered bitterly.

'What made you so mad that you hit him so hard?' she questioned.

'I don't like being teased.'

'You know you seriously hurt him, don't you?'

'Yeah. I'm sorry I did, but he deserved it.' Bruce stated as he looked defiantly at Jenny.

Then Bruce looked down at the floor, but it was clear that he didn't really understand the line he had crossed when he harmed Mark so severely.

The next day, Russ phoned Jenny. He was in a rage. 'How dare you tell the doctor about what's happening? He phoned me and almost insisted that I change my idea about Bruce and his crazy pills.'

'You didn't see Mark, or you would know what kind of a rage Bruce was in. Mark has four stitches in his lip, has a cut to his tongue and two of his teeth are loose. He was lucky they weren't knocked out by the force of the blows.'

'It's about time Bruce cleaned his clock! That beating has been a long time coming if you ask me.' he thundered.

Jenny realised that Russ was not going to even attempt to change his mind and realised that it was senseless to talk further with him. 'I have nothing more to say to you Russ. You're obviously not thinking about what's best for both boys.' she hung up.

In a few minutes Mark came downstairs. His face was as white as death. 'What's the matter Mark?' she asked.

'I heard Dad. I heard what he said,' as he struggled to talk with his sore mouth. 'I hate him. I hate him. He always wants Bruce and me to fight and gets mad when I won't fight. He calls me a sissy. I don't want to ever stay with him again!'

She reached for him and gave him a gentle hug. 'I think because you're almost thirteen, you're old enough now that the courts won't force you to go with him. I'm going to phone them tomorrow to see what we can do about this.'

She walked him back upstairs and tucked him in and soothed his brow until he fell asleep again.

When Bruce saw the psychiatrist, Jenny explained the problems she was facing with Russ and how Bruce reacted when he was off his medication.

'Let me talk with Bruce for a while and I'll see what's going on with him.' he recommended.

Jenny sat in the waiting room wringing her hands. She knew her family was in trouble and that something had to be done about it. When the doctor returned to the waiting room, he beckoned to Jenny to follow him as he said, 'Bruce you stay here. There are some good comic books over there you can read.'

The doctor said, 'I think we should do an electro-encephalogram with Bruce. It will show whether there is any unusual brain activity. His problem might not just be hyperactivity. It could be something else. Has he had any serious falls? Any very high fevers when he was a child?'

Jenny recalled the electric shock she had received before he'd been born and told the doctor about it.

'That might have made a difference. We will know much more after we've completed the test. Why don't I see when it can be done and we'll have more information upon which to base our treatment.'

Two days later, Bruce had the tests. Jenny stayed in the room. The doctor explained what the suction cups holding the wires were for, as he placed them on Bruce's head. Bruce didn't seem frightened, just interested in the procedure. The doctor assured them both that the test was painless and that it just recorded the brainwaves in Bruce's head.

When the doctor examined the test results, he spoke with Jenny. 'These tests show that Bruce has a brain disorder likely caused before he was born.'

'Do you think it was caused by the electrical shock he had?' she asked.

'That seems to be the most likely reason.' he agreed.

'How is that treated?' Jenny asked.

'He'll be put on Ritalin, an amphetamine that has helped children with this problem. I don't like to prescribe this medication for purely hyperactive behaviour but have found it calms down the brainwaves in children like him.'

So, Bruce began taking Ritalin and the change in his behaviour was astounding. He did well at home and at school and was a much happier boy. The only continuing glitch was the two days each second weekend when he stayed with Russ.

Jenny had asked that a family study be done because Mark didn't want to see his father and now that she had the report from the psychiatrist, wanted the courts to force Russ to ensure that Bruce took his medication.

A week later, the social worker conducted the home study with Jenny and the children. She spoke with Mark about his distaste for his father and why he didn't want to see him any more. She also spoke with Bruce to see why he wasn't taking his medication when he visited his father. Then she told Jenny that she would be doing a further home study the next Saturday when it was Russ's turn with the boys. She promised that she would make a ruling ten days after that.

Jenny held her breath thereafter and was both anxious and apprehensive when the social worker asked her to come to her office. The social worker said she had evaluated what was going on with the family, encouraged Jenny and Russ to bury their differences, but did not change the court order. Mark was still expected to visit with his father every second weekend and Russ had been encouraged to ensure that Bruce took his medication while he was there.

Russ's next time with the boys was in two days. Jenny took Mark aside and told him what the courts had decided – that he had to go with his father. 'I'll go, but I'm going to tell Dad what I think of him. I still hate him so much. But I don't want to cause trouble for you Mom, so I'll go.'

She spoke to Bruce as well, 'Honey, the courts say that your Dad is supposed to make sure you take your medicine. They will make him do that, so I want you to promise me that you will take your medicine this weekend.'

'Okay Mom. I'll take my medicine with me.' Jenny noted that he had not promised to take that medication, just take the medication with him.

That weekend Russ had a long private talk with Bruce who was now eleven years old. He said that he wanted Bruce to live with him. If Bruce moved in with him he promised he would have a room or his own, and Russ would buy him a new bike. When Bruce came home on Sunday, he told Jenny about his conversation with his father.

'What do you want to do?' Jenny asked apprehensively.

'I think I will do it. I'll move in with Dad.' was the unexpected answer.

'Are you sure that's what you want to do? What about your brother and sister? Won't you miss them?'

'Mark will have his own bedroom if I live with Dad. He won't have to share it with me any more, so it will be good for him too. And they will visit every second weekend.'

'Did your Dad want Mark and Debbie to come too?'

'I don't know whether he talked to Mark or Debbie.'

Later Jenny asked Mark whether his father had spoken with him. 'I didn't say a word to Dad the whole weekend. No, he didn't talk to me. Why do you ask?'

'Your Dad has asked Bruce to live with him and Bruce has agreed to go.'

'I guess that's his decision, but I will never want to live with Dad. I hate him. I don't think he spoke with Debbie either, otherwise she would have told me.'

The next Wednesday, all the plans were in place for Bruce to move in with Russ. Bruce and Mark had gone through their toys and had divided them up, so Bruce could take his with him. On the day when Russ came to pick him up and after Bruce was settled in the van, Russ took Jenny aside and renewed his vendetta against her, 'I have the house, the cottage, the car, the bank account and now I have Bruce. You're going to end up with nothing!' he spat at her.

After Bruce had gone, Jenny just sat there with Mark and Debbie. She knew she couldn't take much more of this. That night she phoned Ian and Martha in Victoria to discuss the situation with them. Jenny decided that she had to leave Winnipeg; that she couldn't take any more of the tension of living in the same city as Russ. She knew he meant his vendetta and didn't want to give him the opportunity of taking Mark and Debbie away from her.

As expected, Martha said, 'Come here to Victoria. You know you're welcome here anytime.'

'No Mom, this is something I need to do on my own. It seems that there is lots of work in Alberta. I think I'll go there and see if I can't get a job.'

'Whatever you want dear but know you can always count on us to help out if you need us.' Martha added.

It was summer holidays, so Jenny packed Mark and Debbie in the car and started driving westward. Mark was now almost thirteen and Debbie was six. When Jenny and her family got to Calgary, Alberta she rented a motel and purchased several local newspapers. Then she scoured the want ads and found an advertisement for a legal secretary. She phoned the office and was offered an appointment for that afternoon. Mark agreed to look after Debbie while she was gone.

At the interview, Jenny met the lawyer, Mr. Ruby and was pleased to learn that he was also from Winnipeg. He specialised in finalising home real estate sales. Jenny had kept her typing skills up but was quite rusty in the shorthand area. They hit it off right away and he offered her the job.

'I'll have to return to Winnipeg for two weeks or so, but as soon as I can find a place to stay and to move my belongings, I could start.'

'Have you found a place to rent?' he asked.

'Not yet, but I'll get busy looking as soon as I get back to my motel.'

'As you know, I'm associated quite closely with the real estate market. I know of a place that might suit you and your two children. Why don't I call the lady who owns the place and see if she can let you see it today.' he replied.

'That would be wonderful. How kind of you to save me that trouble.'

Jenny and the children examined the home he recommended and were pleased with it. The rental unit was the upstairs of a two-storey home. It had a living room, dining room, kitchen and three bedrooms. The landlady, who introduced herself as Nancy Kelly, was an elderly widow who lived in the lower unit. When she finished showing Jenny around the unit, she said, 'If you rent the unit, I would be able to keep an eye on the children both before and after school while you worked.'

Jenny glanced at the children and they both nodded. They already liked the kind lady who would live in the same home as they.

'Would we be able to park our tent trailer in the back yard?' asked Jenny.

'That would be fine, there's lots of room to park the trailer and our two cars in the back.'

'That would be wonderful. I'd like to rent the unit to start in two week's time, the 15th of August. We'll be back then in time for me to start work. Where is the nearest school for the children? Mark will be in junior high school and Debbie will start Grade one.'

Nancy got out the phone book and looked up the phone number of both schools. Jenny talked to both school administration staff and enrolled her children for the start of the school year in September. She knew that she would have to obtain Mark's school records from his present school in Winnipeg but didn't think that would be a problem. Because this was Debbie's official first year in school, she didn't have any school records to collect. Although the schools were two blocks apart, she arranged for Debbie to stay at the school until Mark could come and collect her. He would also be able to walk Debbie to school in the morning.

It all happened so quickly and smoothly, that Jenny knew she'd made the right decision to move to Calgary and start a new life for her family. That night she phoned Ian and Martha with the good news and the next day drove back to Winnipeg.

At home, Jenny ordered a moving truck to come the next Monday and they all began packing boxes. She went to the school and obtained Mark's school records then informed the family court workers that she would be moving with Mark and Debbie to Calgary. She was tempted to phone Bruce to give him her new address, but the last thing she wanted Russ to know was exactly when she would be leaving. Instead, she decided that it would be better to give Bruce that information later when they were settled in Calgary. Jenny planned to invite him to join them, so the children could be together again.

On Thursday evening Jenny spotted Russ's van cruising along their crescent and knew that the family court worker must have told him about their pending move. Jenny phoned her parents and asked them what she should do.

'We're coming. Just keep packing and we'll be there as soon as possible.'

Ian and Martha left Victoria early the next morning, took the ferry with their car to Vancouver then drove continuously to Winnipeg – changing drivers every two hours.

As soon as they arrived on Sunday afternoon, they advised Jenny to pack the kids in the car and go. Jenny had almost completed the packing by then. Ian helped Jenny put the trailer on the hitch and off they went. By midnight that night Jenny, Mark and Debbie had crossed the Saskatchewan border and were heading for Calgary.

Their furniture would not arrive until Wednesday, so Jenny and her children slept in their trailer as they passed through Saskatchewan the first two nights. One of the campgrounds had a swimming pool and they all had a lovely afternoon relaxing by the pool. Jenny decided they should arrive in Calgary Tuesday night, so they'd be there early in the morning for when the moving truck arrived. That night, they took their sleeping bags and air mattresses from the trailer and slept on the floor of their apartment. Nancy Kelly insisted that they have breakfast with her that morning.

In Winnipeg, the moving truck had arrived to pick up their belongings on Monday morning. Shortly after the van left with the furniture, Ian and Martha were standing outside the unit, preparing to return the keys to the resident manager, when a woman walked up to them.

'I'd like to speak with Mrs. Carponi.' she requested.

'I'm sorry she's not here,' Martha replied.

'I have a court order banning her and the children from leaving the province.' the woman said as she tried to hand Martha the document.

Martha stepped back refusing to accept the document. 'You'll have to come back another time if you want to serve it. Mrs. Carponi is not here.'

Her parents chuckled as they drove towards Calgary. They stopped at a motel along the way and had a well-deserved rest and reached Jenny and the children's new home in Calgary on Wednesday, just after the moving truck arrived.

They all pitched in and soon had everything unpacked and settled. Ian repaired a few things in the apartment then he and Martha returned to Victoria a couple of days later. Jenny started her job the next Monday leaving Nancy Kelly in charge of the children for the ten days before they were to start for school.

Jenny and her children started a new life, finally free from Russ's tyranny – at least so she thought ...

The summer Bruce turned sixteen, Jenny was surprised to hear his voice on the phone. 'Can I come for a visit?' He asked.

'Of course!' she almost shouted.

So, that summer Bruce visited Jenny, Mark and Debbie then went back to Winnipeg to finish his schooling. When he was nineteen, Jenny was able to find him an apprenticeship position as a heavy-duty mechanic with the company she was working for. Bruce accepted the position, but within six months missed his friends so much in Winnipeg that he rented an apartment and moved back to be with his boyhood friends.

Bruce married Carlie in 1992 and their daughter Carolyn was born in 1999. The three of them lived in Winnipeg near Russ and spent time with him on a regular basis.

In 1982 Jenny had opened her international training firm and in 1998 immigrated to Australia to be nearer to her Asian clients. She realised that as she was getting older, her chances of falling on the ice in Canada became more of a hazard. However, she visited her children and grandchildren in Canada twice a year thereafter.

In early 2009, Bruce was having problems with his right shoulder and in June, he sent Jenny the following e-mail:

> Hello. I went for further tests today at the neurologist. Sit down before reading further. It is not good news. They are about 97% sure that I have Lou Gehrig's disease as they call it in the USA (ALS as they call it in Canada and Motor Neuron Disease in Australia). They are waiting for a couple more tests; a third MRI on my brain this time. We have not told Carolyn anything yet! I am still off work until further notice; if I go back at all. I will update as we know further information.

Soon the diagnosis was confirmed. Jenny couldn't help but wonder if the shock Bruce received before he was born, had resulted in him having this horrible disease. Again, she felt great animosity towards Russ, who she felt could be responsible their son's illness.

Motor Neuron Disease paralyses a person bit by bit, until they can't move a muscle. In most cases this can take three to ten years to progress to the final stages. However, Bruce degenerated very quickly and within seven months was in a palliative care unit hardly able to move and was fed with a tube in his stomach. Jenny made a trip to Winnipeg in July 2009 shortly after he was diagnosed and then again that Christmas.

On May 24th, 2010 she was sitting at her computer in Australia when she had the sudden realisation that she needed to go to Canada as soon as possible. Her flight arrived on May 29th and she was able to visit with Bruce for the next three days and was able to say her final goodbye just before he died on June 2nd.

The next day, Jenny received the stunning news that Russ was paying for the funeral and was banning her from attending it. She was booked to return to Australia on June 8th so there was plenty of time for her to go to his funeral, but Russ booked the funeral for June 9th. She realised that he was still fulfilling his vendetta and was still hurting her by not letting her say her final farewell to her son. She couldn't believe he could be so cruel and tried to find out why Bruce's wife Carlie was allowing Russ to make these decisions about his burial.

But Carlie kept her phone on answering service and refused to talk to Jenny. Jenny even tried sending e-mails to Carlie asking to see Carolyn on the weekend before she flew home to Australia, but there was no reply, so she was denied such a visit. And, she was completely devastated emotionally because Mark and Debbie did nothing to stop their father from following through with his plan.

When Jenny returned to Australia, all the e-mails she sent to Carlie and Carolyn were returned because they must have obtained new e-mail addresses. This she knew was due to Russ's continued influence and interference.

Not only was she cut off from her granddaughter Carolyn, but she seldom received any correspondence from Mark or Debbie. She felt that they had gone over to the enemy camp and vowed that she would not return to Canada until she was invited by one of them.

She waited two years for such an invitation, but it did not come. In July, 2012 Jenny realised that she was punishing herself by not going back to Canada to see her many friends and cousins. So, she contacted her friend Adele in Winnipeg and asked if she could visit. Adele was relieved that Jenny had made that decision. Jenny normally stayed with Mark when she went to Edmonton, but seeing she had not been asked to visit, she simply sent an e-mail to Mark telling him she was coming to Canada. If he had not replied, she would have arranged to stay with her friend Adele.

His return message was a relief because he invited her to stay with them. Jenny agonised about what she was going to say to Mark when she arrived. She was still so hurt by his seeming defection to the enemy – leaving her isolated in Australia.

She wondered how she could explain her agony. It was several days into her visit before she had the opportunity of speaking with him privately. She decided to start by asking, 'What do you think is the best way for me to try to see Carolyn. I've been completely cut off from her since the day Bruce died, but I want to see her to let her know that I still care about her.'

Mark replied, 'I don't think you will be able to see her.'

Jenny looked at him closely and replied, 'Why?'

'Dad is still interfering.'

'What right does your dad have to keep me from seeing my granddaughter?'

'Carlie is scared stiff of him and will do anything he says she should do – just the way she acted when she was married to Bruce. Bruce was the boss of that family and now dad has taken over.'

Then she asked, 'Why was I banned from attending the funeral?'

Mark's reply was, 'Dad was too fragile to have you there.'

When Jenny questioned him on why he would be too fragile, Mark's reply was, 'He is still furious at you because you left him in 1971.'

Jenny was fuming. 'Do you have any idea what kind of bastard your father really is?'

Mark sat silently just listening.

'Do you remember the day that Bruce went to live with your Dad?'

'Not really.'

'Do you know why Bruce went to live with him?'

'Not really.'

'Well your dad bribed him with a room of his own and a new bike! He didn't really want Bruce – he just didn't want me to have him!'

'Do you remember all the cards, letters and gifts we sent to Bruce after we moved to Calgary?

'Yeah, but he never answered.'

'Do you know why he didn't answer them? It's because your dad did not give any of them to him, nor did he let me talk to him on the phone. What a cruel thing to do to Bruce! He thought we had deserted him, when we had every intention of bringing him to Calgary as soon as we were settled.'

She also reminded him that his father had deserted him too and did not contact him or his sister for four long years. 'Now that's desertion! So, who is the villain here? And why am I being punished by the entire family when I have done nothing wrong?'

'Your dad is a cruel, vindictive man.' Jenny's cheeks were beat red as she recalled the mean things Russ had done to her.

'Do you know what he said to me the day Bruce moved in with him?'

Mark shook his head.

'He renewed his vendetta to me. Yes – he had sworn one on me when I asked for a divorce in 1971 and renewed it when he picked up Bruce in 1973. This time he said, 'I have the car, the house, the cottage, the bank account and the kid's education fund – and now I have Bruce. Pretty soon I will have Mark and Debbie and you will have nothing!'

Jenny was sobbing by now as she added, 'That's why I had to take you two to Calgary – otherwise he would have taken you from me as well. And two years ago, he renewed the vendetta he swore at me in 1971 by banning me from attending Bruce's funeral. So, for 39 years he has continued to plan his revenge on me. Well it worked – I was a basket case for two months when I got home to Australia.'

She and Mark had a long discussion where she outlined many of the cruel and vindictive things his father had done while they were married.

Jenny was sad that Mark did not comment much through this conversation, but she hoped that he was absorbing everything she was saying. Her greatest wish was that he would resume a regular e-mail or SKYPE correspondence with her in the future.

Her next Canadian stop was Winnipeg where she attempted to see Carolyn who was now thirteen. She had learned from neighbours that Carlie was at work and Carolyn was at home alone, so she knocked on both the front and back doors. She did not see Carolyn but knew that she was ignoring her by refusing to answer the door. Whether this was voluntary or whether she had been warned not to speak to Jenny didn't matter – Jenny was not going to see her and realised that if she phoned, she would get the answering machine as usual.

Time would only tell whether things would improve, and she would be loved and cherished again by her son, daughter and grandchildren.

In early January of 2009, Jenny learned that Russ had been in an accident. His truck had hit black ice and had rolled several times down an embankment. His neck was injured, and he ended up in a wheelchair. Jenny couldn't help but think to herself, 'Now you know what it feels like and I hope you receive the same non-care from your wife as you gave to me when I was in a wheelchair.'

Russ remained in his wheelchair until he died on Christmas day of 2013. The vendetta was finally over.

www.ingramcontent.com/pod-product-compliance
Lightning Source LLC
Chambersburg PA
CBHW051239250626
47155CB00009B/3095